FAIR EXCHANGE

MR LATIF'S GAME

ISBN: 0615743692

ISBN 13: 9780615743691

SYNOPSIS

Renee, the promiscuous daughter of Lillian and Charlie Morningstar, only goal in life is monetary gain. Lillian, a crossing-guard by day supplements her income by selling boot leg corn liquor and serves as the back bone of her family. Charlie, her husband, a retiree from the Steel Mill Company after having worked 26 years is a compulsive alcoholic. Charlie, who is of Native American descent passed his distinctive features to his daughter Renee. With long jet black hair, hair cheekbones and a caramel complexion she is a force to be reckoned with and refuses to let anyone knock her hustle including her three children. Because she prefers the concrete jungle, over parenthood her only son Kevin gets introduced to the drug game by Twin a young Boss who embraces him as a brother then becomes his mentor. However, Twin's life is cut short when he's murdered during a robbery that he had no knowledge of nor did he play a part in. Will Twin's death be swept under the rug, or will retribution be a fair exchange?

PREFACE

"For what shall it profit a man if he gain the world but lose his soul?" John the Baptist yells. As he approaches the small group of men on the corner, he is followed by a deafening barrage of shotgun fire.

ACKNOWLEDGMENT

Money Russ (Justice), thanks for your support and patience. You're definitely a true blue brother. I really appreciate you being there for me.

Kyle Searcy, I love you from the bottom of my heart to the balcony of my brain. Come home, son. I need you.

Rosetta and Colwill Chatman, this work wouldn't have been possible without y'all. I love y'all deeply.

Linda Cooks (Brick House), words aren't enough to explain how deeply in love I am with you. You know how we get down and stay down. See you soon, honey. Chat Daddy, you're everything. I am lying for you like a dirty rug.

DEDICATION

This work of fiction is dedicated to my sister, Linda Chatman, and my first cousin, Michael Grant. May you both rest in peace. Man, I miss you both so much that nothing in this whole wide world can equate to my grief when it concerns you two.

CHAPTER 1

CHICAGO-1982

"Kevin, wake up! Come on, Kevin. Get up!" Libby shouted urgently while simultaneously shaking him awake.

"Stop! Get off me. Leave me alone!" Kevin barked from beneath the thick comforter.

"Boy, you better get up. Now, Kevin," Libby yelled. She snatched the comforter completely off the bed, leaving Kevin's frail little body exposed. Kevin was curled up in the fetal position with one sock on and the other missing. He was also sporting his favorite Batman drawers.

"Where's Renee at?" Kevin asked, sitting up in bed. He was lethargic, upset, and sort of confused from having his sleep abruptly disturbed.

"I don't know where Renee's at. She was gone when I woke up. Now get out that bed. We finna go to Grandma's house."

"Where we finna go?" Kevin asked, wiping sleep from his eyes.

"To Grandma's house. I ain't gon tell you no more. Now put on our jamas so we can leave. Deyla, you ready?"

"Yes, Libby. I'm ready," Deyla responded as she made her way out of the bedroom she shared with her sister, Libby. Unlike Kevin, Deyla was eager to get out of the house. Excitement replaced fatigue in the anticipation of going to Grandma Lillian's house.

"Is Renee going with us?" asked Deyla.

"Nah, she ain't going with us," Libby snapped. She wasn't in the mood for questions. Libby had a zillion thoughts racing through her young mind. It would be their first time going to Grandma Lillian's house without the supervision of their mother, Renee. To make matters even worse, it was well past midnight and frigid as the inside of a dead hoe's pussy outside.

Libby had awakened to find that Renee, for the umpteenth time, was missing in action. Fed up with her mother's antics, Libby decided to take her brother and sister to the house of the one person she knew wouldn't forsake them. Grandma Lillian. "Kevin, if you don't hurry up, we gon leave you in this house by yourself," Libby lied. She was operating on nervous energy and anxious to start the formidable task of getting her siblings safely to their grandma's house.

"I'm coming!" Kevin yelled from his bedroom.

"*Now,* Kevin," Libby shouted.

For several hours snow flurries had descended from the darkened sky, painting the city's gloomy gray structures milk white. The arctic weather was typical of the Windy City in the wintertime. Nine inches of snow covered the pavement like an enormous white carpet. Traffic was light at two in the morning on a Monday morning. The few mobile cars traveled at a snail's pace. More than likely they were occupied by late-night tricks, who were relentless in their efforts to pay for a shot of pussy. Perhaps, though, they wanted lightning quick blow jobs from the hoes that were still out working and trying to meet their quotas before calling it quits. Some of the nightwalkers huddled around a garbage can campfire like an offensive line, waiting for the next play to be called. Throughout the block some even bunched together in doorways in feeble attempts to generate body heat, but Jack Frost had a plan of his own. Mr. Frost inhaled deeply and blew cold air off Lake Michigan. Propelling snowflakes through the air it caused near-zero visibility for those unfortunate stragglers still out and about. Freezing cold and scared to death, Libby clutched the hands of her two siblings—nine-year-old Kevin and seven-year-old Deyla. The trio struggled against the brutal blizzard en route to their grandmother's house dressed only in pajamas.

When the weather permitted and Renee wasn't busy running the street, she would occasionally take the kids the short distance from Forty-fourth and Calumet to Forty-fifth and King Drive, to her mother Lillian's house. Libby navigated her way through the snow. When they reached the corner with the huddled prostitutes, Libby picked up her pace. She moved with only the thought of making it safely to Grandma Lillian's house.

Lillian had finally drifted off to sleep. Sleep was always difficult for Lillian, especially after fighting with Charlie, her. Charlie Morningstar was a small man of Native American descent. He was officially retired from the Chicago Steel Mill Company after working twenty-six years with the company. The majority of his time now was spent in front of the television watching sports in his personal chair, where he even had his meals delivered to him. When Charlie was sober, he was the most pleasant person one ever wanted to meet. When he was drinking, though, which was all the time, he was the exact opposite. Today Charlie was the opposite. He called his liquor fire water, and whoever came by the house when he'd been drinking would more than likely get burned. Charlie couldn't handle his liquor, but he didn't allow that to stop him from drinking. He would get so belligerent when he drank, his wife would have to physically subdue him sometimes. Lillian called the shots She had a dark complexion with huge breasts and thighs close to three hundred pounds. This was in stark contrast to her husband's frail one hundred fifty-pound frame. Lillian was a crossing guard by day, but when the sun went down, she operated a bootleg distillery from her house.

Lillian returned home from church, set her pocketbook down on the stand, and began to remove her coat when Charlie, yelled, "Lillian, is that you?" Lillian could tell right away Charlie was drunk by his slurred words.

"Yeah, it's me. Who did you think it was, your dead mama?" said Lillian. She didn't feel up to dealing with his drunkenness. The fight broke out during the football game. The Chicago Bears were playing the New England Patriots. The Patriots were on top 23–21. It was the fourth quarter with thirty seconds left on the clock. The Chicago Bears had possession of the ball and were attempting to kick a field goal from the forty-five yard line when Mr. Charlie, in a drunken stupor, decided to let off some steam. He began to yell obscenities at the TV. "Kick the fucking ball, you Yankee cocksucker. Hurry up and kick that motherfucker. I gotta go take a piss god damn it." Charlie was standing in the middle of the room, struggling to maintain his balance. Thick, frothy foam of saliva was caught in the corner of his mouth. He was gripping the crotch of his pants.

Lillian was in the kitchen preparing a meal when she heard Charlie barking obscenities. Lillian went to the front room to investigate the situation. When she got to the threshold of the room, she stopped in her tracks. She was momentarily startled at what she witnessed. Then her blood began to boil. Charlie was swaying back and forth in front of the TV with his dick protruding from the open zipper of his pants. He was sporting a huge, Kool-Aid smile on his twisted, intoxicated face as he released his bladder in the front room. It looked as if he was trying to put out an invisible fire. Piss was all over the television. The only exception, of course, was his personal chair.

"Bitch-made motherfucker," Lillian yelled at the top of her lungs. She charged forward with the momentum of a raging bull, head down and feet stomping. When Lillian came to her senses, the first thing she noticed was Charlie lying beneath her. Both arms were flailing in the air in a desperate attempt to catch his breath. Lillian had cut off his oxygen supply with the full impact of her three hundred-pound frame.

In Lillian's dream she had finally saved enough money to escape the slum of the ghetto, leaving behind the awful roach- and rodent-infested apartment she had called home for over a decade. As she slept peacefully in her new house in South Holland, Illinois, a Chicago suburb, the chime of the doorbell jolted her awake. Lillian tiredly glanced over at the alarm clock on the nightstand. It read 2:15 a.m. reluctantly she got out of her warm, comfortable queen-size bed, put on her slippers and robe, and proceeded to the door. "I wonder who the hell is ringing my bell at this hour," she thought. "Probably an alcoholic. Who else could it be at this time of morning?" Lillian peered through the peephole but didn't see anyone. Anxious to get back in bed, Lillian thought whoever was at the door must have changed his or her mind and left. But before she could make it back to bed, the bell rang again.

Puzzled, Lillian approached the door and looked through the peephole again. She shouted, "Who the hell is it?"

"It's me, Grandma," Libby cried. Lillian cracked the door with the chain attached and couldn't believe the sight before her. Standing in the hallway of her building were her daughter, Renee's, three children. They were shivering cold and completely covered in snow.

CHAPTER 2

Twenty-four-year-old Renee Janet Morningstar stood five foot eight and weighed one hundred thirty-five pounds. The majority of that weight was in Renee's chest and hips. Her complexion was the hue of coffee with extra cream. Renee's jet-black, shoulder-length hair was the same color as her eyes, which had beautiful, long eyelashes. Her high cheekbones recalled her father's Native American heritage. Renee was bowlegged with a small waist and an incredibly proportioned backside that could be seen from any angle. Her frame was impeccable. Men and women both found Renee irresistible. Renee only had an eighth-grade education, but what she lacked academically, she possessed in street smarts. Besides being an official ghetto cover girl, she was savvy as well.

Jerry's after-hours spot was packed to capacity, as usual, with hustlers. The only requirement for admittance was a ten-dollar cover charge and, of course, recognition of the doorman. Marvin Gaye's voice could be heard blaring through the speakers and permeating the entire joint. "Mother, mother, mother, there's too many of us crying. Brother, brother, brother, there's far too many of us dying. You know you got to find the way to bring some lovin' here today. Hey, what's going on?"

On the tip of her toes, Mimi crept up behind Renee's chair. Mimi placed her hands over Renee's eyes and kissed her on the side of her neck. "Bitch, didn't I tell you to stop putting your soup coolers on me? I'm gonna start charging your ass for kissing on me," Renee huffed.

"Bitch, stop tripping. You know I love you, and I'm gonna sweat you until I get you," laughed Mimi.

"Whatever," responded Renee.

"Girl, I tried to call you before I came out, but you didn't answer your phone, so I figured I'd find you here at Jerry's. What's up? Do you want another drink?"

"Yeah, a double shot of Tanqueray, thank you," said Renee. Mimi had been sweating Renee ever since their first encounter at Nate's Fur Factory. Mimi was bisexual and a professional booster. One afternoon, while Mimi was out plying her trade at Nate's Fur Factory, she spotted Renee trying on a full-length mink coat.

"Damn that bitch is fine," Mimi thought.

"Excuse me," Mimi said, "whoever made that coat must've had you in mind when he designed it. If you want it, I'll give it to you for half price."

"Oh really?" Renee muttered.

"Absolutely," Mimi replied.

"Are you serious?" Renee questioned. It was hard to believe someone she didn't know from a hole in the wall would sell her a ten thousand dollar mink for half price.

"I wouldn't waste your time or mine if I wasn't serious," said Mimi.

"Why do I have the feeling if I accept your offer, I'll end up paying more for the coat than it's actually worth? Not to mention I don't know you from a pot of piss," said Renee, looking Mimi up and down.

"Well, to be honest, from the moment I spotted you trying on that beautiful coat, I wanted you to know me." Mimi extended her hand and introduced herself. "My name is Mimi. What's yours?"

"Renee."

"Pleased to meet you, Renee."

"I'm sure you are" Renee says sarcastically

"Can I ask you something?"

"I'm listening," said Renee, simultaneously taking the coat off and folding it over her arm.

"Have you ever seen a person, place, or thing that had the ability to attract your attention? And the longer you paid attention, the more irresistible it became until the only logical thing was to possess that special person, visit that special place, or purchase that special thing, even if you couldn't afford it, had to put it on layaway, or work two jobs? Have you ever felt that way about something or someone?"

"Of course," Renee exclaimed. "Girl, you just explained how I feel about this coat. I must have this mink."

"I know," Mimi uttered, gazing at Renee as if she was starving, and Renee was a Philly steak sandwich. "But I was also explaining how I feel about you. I must have you. You are gorgeous. If beauty was a minute, you would definitely be an hour. I don't make it a habit of extending myself to strangers. Normally I follow my mind instead of my heart. That way I don't expose myself to unforeseen danger by going against the grain. But all relationships or friendships entail some risk. Right?"

"True," responded Renee.

"And, girlfriend," Mimi continued, "we both know, after our business here is complete, there's no way you will allow me to walk out of your life without the possibility of ever seeing me again."

This was Renee's first time ever being hit on by another woman. Renee stood there in Nate's Fur Factory, intrigued. Renee stared at Mimi's cocoa butter complexion. She was a Halle Berry look-alike, and a sly smirk appeared on Renee's pretty face before responding. "You know what? I had yet to meet a female who persuaded me to step outside the box. But honestly you have piqued my curiosity. Not only am I flattered, I'm also interested," said Renee, handing the mink coat to the Halle Berry look-alike. "Handle your business, girl. I'm parked outside by the exit. I'm driving a red convertible Corvette. Hurry up. My time is valuable."

That first encounter at Nate's Fur Factory gave birth to a seriously flirtatious friendship between the two women.

"Jerry, give my girl a double shot of Tanqueray, and I'll have my regular," said Mimi.

"Cheap bastard should give us those drinks on the house," Renee whispered. "All the money we spend in this shit hole. Not to mention what I blew in the back on the craps table before you arrived." Renee pouted in disappointment.

"Bitch, say word," snapped Mimi.

"Word." Renee smirked.

"How much, Renee?"

"Something small."

"How small?" Mimi asked.

"Just nine hundred," said Renee.

"Bitch, are you insane?" Mimi barked. "Blowing that kind of money on the craps table. That's fuckin' crazy."

"Easy come, easy go," smiled Renee.

"Well, if you need to hold a few dollars, say something. A closed mouth can't get fed just like a closed book can't get read."

"Thanks, Mi, but I'm good. I was just explaining. I hope you didn't think I was complaining. You know how I get down. Shit, as long as they continue to print it, I'm gonna continue to count it. For the life of me, I can't understand how any bitch would accept being broke in this vast land of milk and honey. Stupid bitches better wake up and realize they was blessed with gold mines."

"Hold up, bitch. I just know you ain't talking about what I think your ass is talking about," said Mimi, taking a sip from her martini.

"Yes, bitch," Renee smiled her infectious smile. "This right here." Renee pointed at her crotch. "It's a gold mine, stupid."

"Girl, yo ass is crazy as hell," laughed Mimi.

"Yeah, well, as long as these weak-ass niggas want to explore my gold mine searching for hidden treasures, I'm gonna charge their asses a fee. On second thought," Renee said, taking a sip of her drink, "I can use a couple hundred."

"Bitch, I thought you said you was good?" said Mimi.

"I am, but I can always use some help," Renee exclaimed. Mimi reached inside her pocketbook and pulled out a stack of large bills. She peeled off three hundred dollars and handed it to Renee. "Thanks," said Renee. Then she abruptly stuck her finger in Mimi's drink and rubbed it across Mimi's full lips. Mimi opened her mouth, but Renee withdrew her finger before Mimi could suck Renee's finger into her mouth. Renee giggled and asked Mimi how many malls she robbed over the weekend.

"Bitch, don't insult me," Mimi barked. "My career started in the mall, but that's not where it ended. I play boutiques. I outgrew malls when I outgrew training bras."

"Well, excuse me, miss thief. Unfortunately some of us still shop at the mall. That reminds me. I need a new outfit for next Saturday. I'm going to the Calvary, and I gotta be fresh."

"Well, miss thing," Mimi said, batting her eyes at Renee. "I just might be able to assist you in that department," Mimi purred. "I stole some fly pieces from Andrew Malley's that I'm sure you'll like."

"What kind of pieces?"

"Some pieces I know you can afford," said Mimi, showcasing her most seductive smile. "Let me see. I took six Dolce and Gabbana silk blouses, three Coach pocketbooks, and this gorgeous three-quarter length turquoise leather jacket. Oh, I almost forgot. I took this hot pink, iridescent pantsuit that I'm sure would look crazy on you."

"How do you know how it will look on me?"

"Because I know how you like to wear formfitting clothes, and this outfit was made to hug your curves like an elastic glove. And bitch, you got more curves than the yellow brick road." Mimi smiled.

"I'm willing to bet you say that to all your female customers," Renee exclaimed.

"Damn, that hurts. You are much more than a customer to me. That's why I'm bursting at the seams to see how that hot pink suit looks on you. I was gonna keep it for myself."

"Too late, bitch. It's already sold," Renee snapped.

"When can you come by my apartment to appraise the merchandise?" asked Mimi.

"Call me, and I'll let you know. Right now I gotta get the fuck outta this trap before I end up broke. I gotta get home to my babies."

"OK, I'm gona have one more drink, and then I'm outta here myself. Be expecting my call, Renee. We just might be able to work something out for that stinky pinky pantsuit," Mimi uttered, slowly licking her lips. She let her hand drop down on top of Renee's fishnet-clad thigh.

Renee removed Mimi's manicured hand, and then stood up and prepared to exit Jerry's after-hours spot. "Mimi," said Renee, looking into her light brown eyes, "you're using the wrong bait to catch me. You need to use monetary instead of material bait. Try it and see how far it gets you. Call me. I'll be waiting."

Renee left Jerry's tired and with a headache. Her feet were killing her from walking around in high heels all night. The only thing on Renee's mind was checking on her children and getting some much-needed rest. Renee stuck her key in the lock, opened the door, and stepped inside her apartment. Once inside, an intense silence greeted her, and she instantly became uneasy and alert. She reached Kevin's room first. It was empty. From the condition of his bed, it was obvious he had slept in it. "Kevin! Kevin!" Renee yelled as she rushed toward Libby and Deyla's bedroom, which was also abandoned. In a pseudo religious fit, Renee suddenly acknowledged the Supreme Being. "Lord Jesus," she shouted, "where are my babies? God, please let them be safe." Renee had left her children home alone on numerous occasions and had always returned to find them either asleep or watching television together. Never had she come home to discover an empty house. In a state of panic, Renee snatched the phone and dialed her mother's number.

"Hello?" said Lillian after the third ring.

"Mama, the kids are missing. I had to make a quick run. I was only gone twenty minutes, and when I got back to the house, the kids was gone."

"Twenty minutes my ass. Who do you think you talking to, Renee? These kids been over here. They were dressed in pajamas in the fucking snow. How they managed is beyond me. Thank god they didn't freeze to death. Renee, listen to me. If something happens to my grandbabies because you'd rather run the streets than stay home with your kids, I'm gonna go to the electric chair for premeditated murder for killing your foolish ass. I swear by god. Now play with me if you want to. If you don't want to raise those kids, then you shouldn't have had them. I don't know where you picked that shit up from, but I know you didn't get it from me," said Lillian. She abruptly slammed the phone down, and the sound rang in Renee's ear.

CHAPTER 3

"Good morning, Libby."

"Morning, Grandma."

"Where are Kevin and Deyla? Are they awake yet?" Lillian asked.

"Nope, they still asleep, Grandma," Libby said as Grandma Lillian went about the business of setting the table. She puts three plates of bacon, eggs, and grits on the kitchen table and poured three cups of orange juice. Lillian folded her arms across her chest and waited for Kevin and Deyla to enter the kitchen so they could eat breakfast. Every time Lillian thought about her grandbabies showing up at 2:15 a.m., she became furious. She could easily strangle her daughter for leaving the kids home alone. Her grandchildren were the highlight of her life. She vividly recollected when Renee was eleven years old, Libby's age. She would seldom let Renee out of her sight. Lillian was old-school. She put God first, then the children, and then herself. The three stooges entered the kitchen, looking like miniature adults. Each took a seat at the table. Lillian's mood changed as she gazed at her grandbabies. The pleasure Lillian derived from their presence was all over her face. Lillian was glowing like a jack-o'-lantern. "Kevin, did you wash your hands?"

"Yes."

"Yes what?" asked Lillian.

"Yes, ma'am," Kevin muttered. Lillian took a seat at the table and watched as her grandbabies demolished breakfast. "Who wants some more breakfast?" Lillian asked.

"Me," Kevin managed through a mouthful of eggs and grits.

"Me too," said Deyla, raising her arm in the air.

"Damn, Renee, these children were actually starving," Lillian thought. She decided right then and there she would relieve her daughter of the duty and responsibility of raising the children. She would raise them herself. That way she wouldn't have to worry about their safety.

"Libby, Kevin, and Deyla, Grandma wants to ask y'all something."

"What, Grandma?" asked Libby.

"Do y'all like being at Grandma's house?" Everyone said yeah in unison. "Would y'all like to live here with Grandma?" Libby and Deyla both answered with another yes. "So be it," Lillian uttered. "Y'all live with Grandma now."

"We do for real?" Kevin asked with a happy expression.

"Yes, Kevin. It's for real, baby. Now can Grandma have a big hug?" Lillian asked as she rose up out of her chair. The kids rushed into the welcoming arms of their surrogate mother.

CHAPTER 4

Unlike Renee, Mimi was educated. She had three years of college under her belt. She'd also worked numerous jobs but was never able to maintain employment. She had been exposed to a lot of illegal activity at a young age. Two of her sisters were outlaws. One of her sisters sold pussy, and the other made a career out of forgery. Their father was doing time in federal prison under the RICO Act. Their mother died from a heroin overdose when Mimi was thirteen years old. Mimi had been raised by her oldest sister, Nicole, who had let Mimi get away with anything. Mimi was both academically smart and street smart. She was a thief, a booster, by trade. Being the youngest of six sisters, Mimi had been forced into her sisters' hand-me-down clothes. This activated her career in the art of thievery. She was in the ninth grade when she committed her first theft.

One evening after school let out, Mimi decided to go window-shopping downtown in Chicago's loop. With only two dollars and a super transfer to her name , Mimi boarded the CTA bus and got off downtown. After a half hour of window-shopping, Mimi gathered enough courage to enter Benetton's clothing store. Shaking like an epileptic patient having a grand mal seizure, she headed toward the blue jean section. Mimi took a deep breath, reached up, and removed a pair of jeans off the rack. Mimi glanced over her shoulder, and then she stuffed the outfit inside her book bag. Sweating profusely, Mimi made her way to the door on shaky legs. Her heart was pounding like a bass drum. She pushed open the door. Expecting the worst she hesitated momentarily. When nothing happened Mimi walked out of the store, and the rest was history.

Mimi decided on taking a bubble bath instead of a quick shower. She made an apple martini to help her relax while bathing. Mimi set her drink down on the tray, lit three scented candles, and cut the lights off inside the bathroom. The light from the candle projected the erotic silhouette of her young, feminine body on the bathroom wall. She slightly bent her knees to remove her panties. Mimi lifted her right leg over the edge of the bathtub, bracing herself in case the water was too hot. She slowly allowed her toes to make contact with the water and then immersed herself into the hot, bubbly water. Mimi took a sip of the martini, closed her eyes, and rested the back of her head on the tub. Mimi felt extra sexy as she anticipated Renee's arrival. It was the first time since they met that Mimi would have some private time with Renee. The mere thought of being alone with Renee's gorgeous ass made Mimi sigh with erotic expectation. Mimi visualized Renee lying across her queen-size bed spread eagle. She imagined her head buried between Renee's legs. Before Mimi realized it, her left hand was caressing her tits, lightly tugging on her nipples.

Her right hand crept down between her legs. She sunk down in the water, bending both knees and placing one on each side of the bathtub. She opened the lips of her vagina and began to trace soft circles around her erect clitoris, gradually applying pressure on it. Her eyes were completely closed, and her head was slightly tilted to the side. Mimi's hand became a blur. She licked her lips as she enjoyed the sensation of a mounting orgasm. Mimi began to moan softly. She was almost there. It was only a matter of seconds before she would erupt in orgasmic bliss. Her thighs started trembling. Mimi penetrated her wet vagina to the knuckle of her middle finger, triggering a breathtaking orgasm.

Mimi finished what was left of her apple martini and climbed out of the tub. She grabbed a towel and wrapped it around her still-trembling frame. She started toward her bedroom to get dressed and prepared for Renee's arrival, but what she desperately hoped for was a hot, eventful evening.

CHAPTER 5

Mimi snatched the phone after the first ring, expecting the sound of Renee's sexy voice on the other end. When Mimi heard a male's voice, she snapped, "Who the hell is this?"

"It's Bear. What the fuck is the matter with you?"

"Oh, hi, Sugar Bear. Sorry, I'm expecting an important call. That's all."

"Correct me if I'm wrong," said Bear, "but the person you're expecting to call is the same gender as you." Bear chuckled.

"Nigga, that's nothing you should be concerned about."

"On the contrary, it concerns me greatly. You and I both have an abnormal desire for the sweet taste of pussy, but your freak ass don't like to share," Bear barked.

"Fuck you, Bear. I don't have time for your bullshit. I know that's not why you called me. So what's up?"

"Bitch, how the fuck you know that's not why I called? You got extrasensory perception or something? You better muzzle your mouth, or I'll do it for you when I get there."

"What? When you get where?" asked Mimi.

"I'm en route to your crib right now. I'm coming to pick up that leather coat I told you I wanted. You still have it, don't you?"

"I still have it. Can you just…" Sugar Bear hung up before Mimi could finish her sentence.

Sugar Bear was a towering figure. He stood six foot six barefoot. His skin tone was the color of burned brass. He weighed a solid two hundred fifty pounds. The man was chiseled like an Egyptian pharaoh. He'd ruthlessly earned the title of undisputed heavyweight champion of the heroin trade on the South Side of Chicago, where he ruled with an iron fist. The best way to define Sugar Bear was as an arrogant motherfucker.

Bear convinced himself he was smarter and wiser than the colleagues he networked with. Except on TV, he had never seen the inside of a jail cell as an adult. Sugar Bear had done a two-year bid in Saint Charles as a juvenile for selling weed, but he was fortunate to never take a bust as an adult. Bear was born in Alabama, and he had moved to the Windy City twenty-six years before with his parents and three brothers. Bear had been ten years old at the time. He was from a long line of hustlers. His grandfather, Midnight, played a major role in introducing three-card monte, AKA red card, to the people in the south. He'd duped countless suckers. He capitalized on those driven by greed and those who thought they could get something for nothing.

He would also charge renegade hoes without pimps for his protection. He was given the moniker "Midnight" because of his complexion, which was blue black. Midnight was a master fake (con man) with more tricks than a circus dog. He had passed the science of tricking down to both his sons, his brother, and June Bug (Sugar Bear's father), who eventually hipped his son to the game. June Bug used to make Bear stay in his bedroom and practice tossing the red card for hours. Bear used to fall asleep practicing sometimes and dream of the day he would be ready to present his game to the public. Bear kept money in his pocket by selling weed and playing three-card monte, but he always thirsted for more. Bear began to recognize it was bigger than the profit. Breaking suckers on the red card was also therapeutic.

Bear's introduction into the dope game happened unexpectedly. One day a notorious heroin dealer named Buddha, who owned the brownstone Bear lived in, was exiting the building and spotted Sugar Bear sitting on the stoop and tossing the red card.

Buddha stopped and asked Bear what he was doing. Bear said, "Playing three-card monte, the same game played on the bus and trolley. Have you ever seen it played before?"

"Hell naw," said Buddha, immediately interested.

"Let me show you how it goes," Bear said. "Look, it's simple and easy, because it's only three goddamn cards. Pay attention to the rules like they taught you in school. Red you win, and black you lose."

"What they call you?" asked Buddha.

"They call me Bear, Sugar Bear. Who you?" asked Bear.

"I'm Buddha."

"OK, Buddha, check it out. If you pick the red, you win, but if you pick the black, you lose."

"Win what? What the fuck I win?" Buddha asked.

"You win one hundred dollars. But if you pick the black card, you lose one hundred dollars," said Bear.

"Bear, if I pick the black card, trust me, I'm gonna do better than that. I'll give you a golden opportunity to step your game up another notch, so you can touch some real paper."

"Bet," said Bear. He started tossing the cards around and talking shit at the same time. "Screw yo wigs on tight, and watch me go, because you just in time for the talent show. Watch it; chase it; see where I place it. They creep and crawl like a fly on the wall. My job is to hide it, and your job is to find it. Where's the red card? If you didn't see it, then I'll shake it again."

"No, don't shake 'em again. I seen it the first time," said Buddha. He pointed to the middle card, certain it was the red card. When Sugar Bear flipped over the card, Buddha was amazed it was black.

"What the fuck?" Buddha uttered. "Man, I would've sworn in open court on a stack of holy Bibles the red card was the middle card. Let me find out you a muthafuckin' magician.

You had to cheat. I just can't prove it. I got good eyesight." Buddha barked, shaking his head.

"I might bluff you and sometimes beat you, but Sugar Bear will never cheat you." Bear smiled.

"You got a lot of potential, nigga. Come on, take a ride with me so I can pay you. Your life is about to change," said Buddha.

"Whatever you got for me didn't cost me nothing, sucker ass nigga," Bear thought as he followed Buddha…

CHAPTER 6

Her perfectly round buttocks resembled two WNBA basketballs stuffed inside the back of her formfitting dungaree miniskirt. Despite the knee-high lizard boots with six-inch heels, Renee climbed the stairs to Mimi's apartment with the grace of a panther. She rang the bell at the same time Sugar Bear completed his conversation with Mimi. "I hope this bitch is still home. She knew I was on my way over here," thought Renee. "Mimi, it's me. Open the door," Renee yelled, pressing the doorbell again. "Hurry up, girl. I gotta pee."

"Who is it?" Mimi yelled, knowing exactly who it was.

"It's the bitch you fantasize about. The bitch who's responsible for your panties staying wet. Now open the fuckin' door before I pee in your hallway."

"'Bout time," snapped Mimi as she opened the door. Mimi stepped aside, allowing Renee just enough space to enter the apartment. "I was beginning to think you took a wrong turn or something," Mimi pouted.

"Getting lost is the least of my worries," said Renee, flashing her irresistible smile. "Bitch, don't start tripping. Where's the bathroom?" Renee asked, squeezing her legs together.

Mimi pointed Renee in the direction of the bathroom and watched as Renee strolled down the hallway. Mimi became mesmerized at the way Renee's ass cheeks shook while she walked down the hall toward the bathroom. In Mimi's mind, she was watching the equivalent of a plus-size model working the runway. Both of Renee's ass cheeks were swinging like oval pendulums. Mimi was temporarily hypnotized. She entered a dreamlike state, induced by the sway of Renee's incredible backside. Mimi reluctantly shook off the spell and immediately became aware of how wet her panties were. "Damn," she thought. Mimi rushed into her bedroom and quickly discarded her soiled panties. She stepped inside her walk-in closet and started taking out stolen outfits and pocketbooks, laying the items on top of the bed.

"Bitch, pinch me so I know I'm not dreaming," Renee exclaimed upon entering Mimi's bedroom. "Bitch, your whole walls are covered with mirrors, even the fuckin' ceiling. Girl, this is some unique shit. I'm impressed. I've never seen nothing like it.

"I knew you would," Mimi proclaimed. She was happy to see Renee was feeling her taste.

"Bitch, you stole all that merchandise?" Renee uttered in amazement, focusing her attention on the expensive items strewn across the bed. "You need to start your own business. Open a boutique or something," Renee said while picking up a black sequin jumpsuit.

"Bitch, are you blind, crazy, or both?" snapped Mimi. "I already have a business, and it's booming. Can't you see I sell top-of-the-line accessories?"

"Stop the bullshit. You're far too intelligent to misunderstand my point."

"Be more specific," Mimi said.

"I'm talking about legitimate business," Renee countered.

"I'm doing just fine with the one I got. You know the saying. If it ain't broke, why fix it?"

"I just can't understand how you do what you do," said Renee, taking a leather Coach pocketbook off the bed and slinging it over her shoulder.

"Look, all you need to understand is that I'm very good at my craft. Do I question your profession?" Mimi huffed. "No, I don't, so please stop questioning mine." Mimi rolled her eyes at Renee and walked to her closet to retrieve some more items.

"Mimi," Renee suddenly called out, "come here. I need your assistance on some fashion tips."

"You having a hard time, baby?" Mimi asked, wrapping her arms around Renee's small waist.

"All these pieces are so fly. It's hard to decide what I want, but I'm open to suggestions." Renee smiled.

"Girl, you know I got you," said Mimi, returning the smile. "I suggest you purchase everything. That way you won't waste your time or mine trying to figure out which piece to buy." Mimi whispered something in Renee's ear and then playfully smacked Renee on her beefy backside.

"That's why I can't stand you. If I had your kind of money, I would be spending it at one of the establishments where you stole this shit from. Instead I'm spending my change at Mimi's black market apartment."

Renee was spared the wrath of Mimi's venomous response by the interruption of the bedroom telephone. Mimi crawled across the garments on the bed to get to the phone. She snatched it after the second ring. "Hello?"

"It's Bear. I'm at your front door."

"I'll be right there." Mimi replaced the phone on its cradle then hopped off the bed. "Damn. I forgot Bear was on his way over here," Mimi yelled loudly as she made her way to the front door.

"Bear who?" Renee yelled to Mimi. "Girl, I just know you ain't talking about the infamous Sugar Bear from the South Side."

"That's the only Bear I know from the end of town," Mimi shot back. When Mimi opened her front door, Sugar Bear's imposing figure towered in the doorway. He resembled a black Incredible Hulk. Bear's huge, athletic body obscured Mimi's vision, blocking out the glare of the hallway light.

"Hi, Bear. Come in. Have a seat."

"I didn't drive over here to have a seat. Where's my leather?" Bear asked, following Mimi to her bedroom. When they reached Mimi's bedroom, Bear's first sight of Renee was her bending over Mimi's bed, closely examining a pair of peach cashmere pants. The first thought that entered Bear's perverted mind was committing sodomy on her, right there on the spot. He couldn't see Renee's face from where he was standing. Nevertheless he was mesmerized by her incredible backside, and he did not give a fat baby's blue, rashy ass what her face looked like. However, when Renee turned around, Bear thought to himself, "Damn, this bitch is drop-dead gorgeous."

"What's up, angel?" Bear asked as he entered the bedroom.

"Angel?" said Renee, looking the Hulk up and down. "That's not my name."

"Well, it should've been," Bear countered.

"And why is that?" Renee replied.

"Because you look like you slipped and fell from up above."

Renee beamed her infectious smile and said, "Flattery will get you everywhere."

"What you doing window-shopping? Or do you plan on making a purchase?" asked Bear, stepping toward the bed to analyze the merchandise more closely.

"A little of both, but I done fell in love with these beautiful cashmere pants," Renee proclaimed.

"I think I done fell in love too," Bear responded. "Are you single and free like me?"

"Yes, I'm definitely single, but I'm not free," said Renee, looking Bear up and down.

Mimi was in the closet looking for the leather coat Sugar Bear had ordered, while her company flirted in the bedroom. Mimi popped out of the closet like a jack-in-the-box with the leather coat in her arms. She smiled at Sugar Bear and said, "That will be six hundred dollars, B-man."

Bear took the coat from Mimi and began to examine it. Satisfied, he reached into his jacket pocket and pulled out a wad of one hundred dollar bills. "Here," said Bear, handing Mimi seven hundred dollars. "When you first let me in, you offered me a seat, which I refused. On second thought I've decided to accept your offer. That extra C-note is for any inconvenience my sudden change of heart may cause." Bear took a seat in the huge leather recliner in the corner of the room and asked Mimi if she had anything to drink.

"Of course." Mimi left the room and returned five minutes later carrying a tray with a pint of Rémy Martin, some soda water, sliced lemons, and three glasses. Mimi poured everyone a drink and passed them around.

"Have you made up your mind, or do you need some professional advice?" Bear asked Renee.

"I'm always open to advice," Renee responded, taking a sip of her Rémy.

"Tell you what I'll do," said Bear. He leaned back in his chair. "For every outfit you model for me, I'll buy it for you."

She set her glass of Rémy on the dresser and switched her hips as she walked over to the bed and snatched outfits two at a time. When she grabbed everything on the bed, she began heading to the bathroom.

"Hold up. Where you going, angel?" Bear asked.

"To the bathroom so I can get changed," Renee responded, as if oblivious to Bear's intention.

"Listen, angel…"

"Renee," she snapped.

"OK, Renee. Let's get an understanding, because understanding, as far as I'm concerned, is the best thing to give or receive. One thing I don't tolerate is a bitch trying to play me. Now correct me if I'm wrong, but do I look like I'm down with the Heinz Catsup Crew? You think I'm slow? You better get the fuck back inside this bedroom and start modeling that shit for me if you want it. Do you have a problem with that?"

"No. Not at all, Mr. Bear. Sugar Bear." Renee smiled sheepishly.

"What about you, Mimi? Do you got a problem with her trying on these outfits for me?"

Mimi was mentally calculating how much she would profit if Bear purchased all the merchandise for Renee. "Hell nah. If she don't mind, why should I?"

"Now that's what I'm talking 'bout," Bear shouted, leaning back in the recliner.

"Bitch, I know your ass ain't shy," Mimi said to Renee in a voice laced with excitement. "What are you waiting for? Come outta them clothes. Take that shit off, girl. Now."

Renee walked back to the bed and dropped the clothes on top. She walked over to the dresser and picked up her drink. She gulped down the whole glass of Remy. Renee set the empty glass on the dresser top and began to disrobe.

Mimi put a Sade tape in the sound system, took a sip from her drink, and watched as Renee took off her blouse. She struggled but managed to pull the dungaree miniskirt down over her thick thighs. She clearly understood the effect her body had on the two spectators, so she decided to maximize the effect. She stood in the middle of the bedroom, slowly gyrating her hips. Renee was naked except for her black silk panties and the black knee-high lizard skin boots.

Bear was overly excited, and he had to remind himself to breathe.

"Damn," Mimi repeatedly mumbled to herself.

Bear downed his drink in a single swallow, got a refill, and then yelled, "Fuck trying on the clothes. They already belong to you, angel every single piece. Listen, I got five hundred dollars apiece if y'all entertain me with a freak show," Bear offered, rubbing and stroking his crotch. Without waiting for Renee to respond, Mimi walked over to Bear and stuck her hand out. Bear counted out one thousand dollars in C-notes and threw the money at her. Mimi wanted Renee just as much as Bear. She turned her back on Bear and rose her dress up over her hips, exposing the fact she wasn't wearing panties. Mimi slowly sank to the floor on her hands and knees and began crawling around and picking up the money until she'd retrieved every single bill. Mimi got off her knees and walked over to the dresser. She placed the bills on the dresser, stepped behind Renee, and wrapped her arms around her waist. "That nigga is ghetto rich," she whispered into Renee's ear, "and he gonna pay like he weigh. Relax, just go with the flow, baby. Let's have some fun at his expense. You only live once."

Mimi stuck her tongue through the loop in Renee's earring, sucking both earring and earlobe into her juicy mouth. Without warning Mimi started spearing her tongue in and out of Renee's ear and simultaneously squeezing her tits and lightly tugging on her erect nipples. Renee spilled some of her drink on the beige carpet. Renee started to tremble. It felt as if her legs were about to collapse underneath the weight of her body. She was on fire.. Renee was a willing participant, though, and couldn't wait to see what would happen next. She didn't have to wait long. Mimi spun her around so they were facing each other. Renee's hard nipples poked Mimi's feminine body as they embraced in a passionate kiss. Mimi palmed Renee's magnificent backside. She made a wet trail down Renee's neck with her long tongue, twirling it around Renee's tiny Adam's apple. Mimi continued down her chest and got poked in the eye by a hard nipple. Horny and out of control with lust, Mimi unleashed a merciless attack on Renee's erect nipples. She flicked her long, wet tongue back and forth across them.

Bear was now stretched out on the recliner beating his dick through the open zipper of his pants. The freak show had just begun, and he was dangerously close to busting his first nut. Pre-come oozed from the head of his dick. He stroked himself up and down as he watched Mimi lick, suck, and fondle Renee's curvaceous body. Mimi smacked Renee on her ass then walked over to the dresser to finish her drink. She motioned for Renee to come help her out of her polka-dot sundress. Mimi lifted both arms while Renee knelt down, grabbed the hem of Mimi's dress, and proceeded to pull it up over her hips. Completely naked, with no shame in her game, Mimi pushed Renee against the dresser and slid her fingers inside the elastic band of Renee's panties. She slowly pulled Renee's panties down her smooth, soft thighs. Renee lifted her legs one at a time so her panties could be removed.

Mimi then helped Renee out of her lizard boots. She tossed them aside. Mimi reached up and took Renee's drink out of her hand, and she dipped Renee's toes in the Rémy. Mimi stuck out her tongue and began to lick Renee's toes.

"Yeah. That's what the fuck I'm talking 'bout. Suck them toes, freak," Bear shouted from across the room.

Mimi set the glass down and then gripped both of Renee's ankles. She started licking and nibbling her way up the inside of those trembling thighs. The closer she got to Renee's pussy, the higher she lifted Renee's legs in the air. Mimi's face was so close to her goal she could smell Renee's woman scent and feel the heat emitting from between her highs. She finally reached her treasure. She inhaled deeply, savoring the tangy aroma exuding from Renee's pussy.

"Breathtaking," Mimi thought with a seductive smile. Her pointy, wet tongue shot out and penetrated Renee's slit, causing Renee's whole body to jerk.

"Ah shit!" Renee responded, almost falling off the dresser. Renee had been busy watching Sugar Bear jerk off when she felt Mimi's tongue suddenly invade her pussy. With her head still buried between Renee's legs, Mimi got up from the floor and forced Renee's body back until she was lying flat on her back with her legs in the air. Mimi positioned Renee so her pussy was at the dresser's edge. Again Mimi's tongue collided with Renee's slit, forcing her puffy lips open. Renee began caressing her own tits, tugging and pulling on both erect nipples, and Mimi continued to flick her tongue lightly on and around Renee's now-swollen clit.

Sugar Bear was now completely insane with lust. His hand was a blur. As he jerked off, he kept repeating the same words "Eat all that pussy. Eat all that pussy." Renee's body trembled uncontrollably from Mimi's torturous mouth and tongue, which effortlessly overpowered her. Mimi raked her manicured fingernails across Renee's soft legs with one hand and twisted and pulled on Renee's nipples with the other.

Renee made low, whimpering sounds, and her eyes were shut. Mimi pushed Renee's legs back farther and started teasing the wrinkle ring of her asshole with her tongue while rubbing her clit with her fingers. "Oh, God," moaned Renee.

Sensing Renee was close to creaming; Mimi revisited Renee's swollen pussy. She plunged her tongue back inside

Renee's wet vagina. That was all it took. Renee started to ramble incoherently. A colossal orgasm seized her. Renee's pussy erupted, releasing female juice all over Mimi's lustful face. Bear was beating his dick as if he'd caught it stealing from him. He had witnessed everything and was now eager to join in on the action. Bear released his dick, reached down, and picked his jacket up off the floor. He took five hundred-dollar bills out of the pocket and wrapped them around his erection. He ordered Renee to come get them. Still recovering from her nerve-shattering climax, Renee made her way across the room on shaky legs, but midway across the room, Bear instructed Renee to crawl the rest of the way. Renee obeyed Bear's instructions without question. Renee dropped to her hands and knees and crawled to the recliner. She stopped between Sugar Bear's big, powerful thighs. Mimi stood in the middle of the bedroom, wide-legged and playing with her pussy. She watched Renee prepare to suck Bear's dick. Bear grabbed a fistful of Renee's hair and pulled her head into his crotch. "I want yo freak ass to suck this five-hundred-dollar sausage real good, angel."

"Well, if you want my best, you gotta let go of my hair so I can have room to work," said Renee.

"I'm not gonna settle for nothing less than yo best," said Bear, loosening his grip on Renee's hair.

Renee removed the money and started polishing Sugar Bear's dick. She wanted to provide the greatest head his money could buy. Renee unbuckled his pants and slid them down to his ankles to get at his dick better, and she ended up getting the surprise of her life. She almost choked when she saw what he was wearing underneath his pants. Bear had on an expensive pair of yellow lace Victoria Secret panties. After the initial shock, she experienced a slight twinge of jealously that she wasn't the proud owner of such a beautiful pair of panties. "I wonder if he's got on the matching bra?" Renee thought. "I should stick my finger up his ass and see how he reacts. Fucking homo thug!"

Renee wrapped her hand around the base of Bear's cock and began to swirl her tongue around the tip. She poked the tip of her tongue inside the oozing open slit on the head of his dick. Slowly Renee engulfed him in her wet, hot mouth until she had the entire erection buried down her narrow throat.

Renee relaxed and flexed her throat muscle to prevent from gagging or choking. Then she proceeded to also take Bear's balls inside her mouth. "Uhm," growled Bear, "angel girl, if this is a demo of your best; I need to sample the worst too." Bear leaned forward and palmed Renee's fat ass cheeks. She continued to bob her head up and down in his lap, and then Renee swallowed him whole. "Goddamn, bitch. Get off me. What the fuck you tryin' to do? Make me come? Slow down, angel. Get off the floor, and sit down on this dick," Bear said, helping Renee up from the floor.

Renee climbed up in Bear's lap with her back against his chest. "Mimi, come over here and help me get this ass pipe inside my pussy."

Mimi danced over to them and dropped to her knees in front of the recliner. She grabbed Bear's dick at the base as if it was a miniature blackjack. She glanced at Renee who was suspended above Bear's lap. "Damn this mutherfucka is huge. You sure you can handle all this meat?" Mimi asked Renee. Renee remained silent.

"Wait your horny ass, bitch. Suck on me a second." Mimi leaned toward Bear, and his dick felt like a piece of steel in her hand. She inhaled deeply, opened her mouth, and stuffed the helmet of Bear's cock inside. Bear shuddered while simultaneously playing with Renee's tits.

"All the way, bitch. Take this cock all the way down your throat." Mimi eased Bear's dick deeper and deeper until she had over half planted in her throat. "Oh my mutherfuckin' God," Bear grunted, looking over Renee's shoulder at Mimi. His dick was stuffed in Mimi's face almost to the hilt. Her eyes were bulging out of her head. "All of it, cocksucker," Bear sneered at her."

Mimi worked hard to get the rest of Bear's cock down her throat. After gagging for the seventh time, she spit the dick out of her mouth. "I can't. It's too fuckin' big," Mimi pouted, stroking Bear's dick up and down. "I hope you ready for this," said Mimi, pushing Bear's stiff cock against the opening of Renee's pussy until the head disappeared between the puffy lips. Renee slowly slid down on Bear, burying his entire erection inside her tight box. Renee felt impaled, so she sat perfectly still until she got accustomed to the feeling. Bear sat still also. He had to adjust to the tight fit of her hot pussy. Renee had one foot planted on each side of the armrest of the recliner. Her knees rested against her chest.

As Mimi began to fondle Bear's balls, she squatted and poked Renee's erect clitoris with her tongue. She lowered her head and took Bear's balls into her mouth one at a time. She attempted to take them both at the same time but failed miserably. Frustrated she grabbed Renee by her waist and bounced her up and down in his lap. Mimi was determined. She waited for Renee to bounce up on Bear's lap, and then she flicked her tongue at the base of his cock. The next time Bear bounced Renee up on his dick; Mimi pulled his dick out and attempted to swallow it again but to no avail.

"Get on the floor with angel," Bear yelled. He stood up in front of the two ladies with his erection pointed in their faces. Bear made them take turns slurping and slobbering on his dick. Mimi sucked Bear off with conspicuous greed. Waiting her turn, Renee glanced down and spotted the yellow panties again. They were tangled around Bear's Timberland boots. Renee immediately got an idea. She crawled behind him, reached between his legs, and started massaging his balls. Mimi kept trying to deep throat him.

"Yeah, play with those balls, bitch. Now lick my ass." Bear was out of his mind with lust. Renee did as she was told. She released his balls, spread his ass cheeks, and stuck her tongue inside Bear's asshole. She stuck her index finger inside her mouth until she was content it was wet enough and then, without provocation, Renee rammed her finger to the knuckle into Bear's asshole. Bear howled like a wounded wolf. "Bitch, I swear on my dead mama, I'm gonna murder your freak ass," he barked, shooting a river of come inside Mimi's mouth.

Mimi gagged and gulped as Bear ejaculated in her mouth. Reluctantly Renee pulled her finger out of Bear's asshole. This was followed by a loud, obnoxious fart that smelled like a decomposed cadaver.

"I'm sorry," Renee frowned. "I got carried away." Renee crawled away from the putrid odor. With a mischievous expression, she took her place next to Mimi. Renee felt a sub-tle sense of victory from the degrading stunt she'd just pulled on Bear. With a wet face and mouthful of come, Mimi leaned toward Renee and gave her a sloppy, wet, intimate kiss, shar-ing Bear's nut with her accepting girlfriend.

"Bitch, you got some explaining to do. Where the fuck you get the heart to stick yo finger up my ass? You think a nigga sweet or something? Huh?"

"Sugar Bear, please don't start trippin'. I just got a little carried away. I'm sorry. When I saw those bright yellow pant-ies wrapped around your ankles, it turned me on, and I just lost it," said Renee with a snide smile on her beautiful face.

Bear glanced down for the first time since Renee low-ered his pants and saw the panties stretched around his boots. He quickly pulled his pants up. When Bear walked out of his house earlier that day, the farthest thing from his mind was getting sexed by two beautiful nymphos, so he hadn't taken the panties off. Bear put on his jacket and snatched the leather jacket he purchased from Mimi off the bed.

"Sugar Bear," Mimi said as she got up off the floor. "Tell me, why are you wearing panties in the first place, big as your dick is?"

"Yo, it's not what y'all think. I'm with you bitches, so it shouldn't be no question about my preference," Bear proclaimed.

"That still doesn't answer my question. Why are you wearing panties?" Mimi pushed.

"Yo, you really wanna know?" Bear said.

"Yes," both women said simultaneously.

"Y'all really wanna know? Because I like the way that shit feels. You only live once, right?" Bear growled, walking out of the bedroom.

Evening had turned into night during the freak session. Renee was now preparing to exit Mimi's apartment. Before Renee said good-bye to Mimi, she told Mimi to show her the iridescent pantsuit.

Mimi went to the closet and retrieved the outfit. She returned, carrying the outfit over her forearm. Renee took it from her and held it up against her body.

"Damn, bitch. You never lied. This fly-ass pantsuit will definitely fit these curves," said Renee. Then she proceeded to fold the outfit and stuff it inside her bag with all the other items Sugar Bear paid for.

"What are you doing?" Mimi asked.

"That question doesn't even deserve an answer. You of all people should know you gotta pay if you wanna play. Bitch, cheer up," Renee said, lifting Mimi's chin. "That's a fair exchange."

CHAPTER 7

SIX YEARS LATER: 1988

"Now y'all niggas know that this dickhead," Twin said, staring at Cee Allah, "can't fuck with me lyrically."

"Nigga, stop bumping your gums. Prove I can't fuck with you. I'll melt yo ass," Cee Allah countered.

"I got a C-note on Twin," said Blob. He reached in his pocket and pulled out a wad of money. He peeled off a one hundred-dollar bill, but no one would give him the bet. Twin hadn't lost a battle yet. Blob was impressed from day one, when he heard Twin spitting fire inside the bathroom at DuSable High School. They both got kicked out of DuSable

High in the last semester of their second year for gangbanging and possession of marijuana.

"Give me a beat, Zulu," Twin barked. Zulu started to beatbox. "Gee whiz, this must be the flip side of show biz 'cause I haven't even started yet, and he startin' to sweat. Who the fuck put this square in our circle? He don't even know how to rhyme yet.

"For years you been walkin' in my shadow. Now you pick me to battle. You ain't gonna do nothing but rattle. Under pressure you probably tattle. I should nip tuck yo Adam's apple, and make you the official homo rapper. Dress you in all red, throw a wig on yo head. Forget about gold or platinum. You lucky to go copper or lead. I was blessed with this gift. I'm obsessed with this shit. I'll lyrically lock on you and shake like a pit, make yo soft ass submit. So you can see how it feels to be verbally bit. Too late for the sad face. Fuck how you look. I ain't shifting the weight. You ain't gettin' off the hook, at least not yet. I just got in yo pussy. I'm tryin' to climax."

"Yo, hold the fuck up," laughed Blob. "How this nigga gone say, let me nip tuck yo Adam's apple and make you a homo rapper? Damn, that was crazy. Yo, Cee, that was slaughter-house style."

"Yeah, that was bananas," Zulu exclaimed.

"Nigga, I always knew you wasn't human. Only a ground-hog can get that low. Kee, Kee, Kee," Blob laughed.

"What the fuck you waiting for, Cee? It's on you. I know you ain't gonna let Twin get away with that nip tuck homo shit he spit at you," Zulu instigated.

"Nah, I got him," Cee Allah said. Zulu began to make music with his mouth again. Cee Allah started to rhyme. "Yo, check it. You more harmless than a toothless wolf. If I see one more feminine trait, I'm gonna snatch yo fuckin' pocketbook. Make you my bottom, bitch. You the homo, mutherfucka. That's why you walk with a switch, you fuckin' closet queen. It's in yo fuckin' genes. Now that you been exposed, why don't you join the stable with the rest of my hoes? Yeah, I picked you to battle. That's why I walked in yo shadow, so I can send you up shit creek without a mutherfuckin' paddle. I got one more suggestion before I end this session. If it's not too much of a hassle, why don't you nip tuck yo own Adam's apple, mutherfucka!"

"Damn!" Zulu exclaimed, pointing at Twin. "He shitted on you, folks."

"It was all right," Blob chuckled, "but that nip tuck shit was authentic. That bar alone left Cee Allah dead in the water."

"How many y'all want?" Lil Kev asked the two approaching dope fiends.

"We tryin' to cop a bundle, but we kinda short."

"Short what, nigga?" Twin intervened.

"We short a pound," said Snaggs, a skinny, tar-colored dope fiend whose facial features resembled a rodent. "You gonna let us cop short five bucks, Twin? You know I am good for it, baby boy." Snot oozed from Snaggs's nose like a broken faucet.

"Good for it? Yeah right," said Twin. "You only good for one thing and one thing only, and that's nothing. You ain't even good at that. Give me that short money, and don't come back until you got my five dollars. Lil Kev, give Snaggs a bundle."

"Thanks, boss man," said Snaggs, nervously wiping snot from his nose with the back of his hand. Lil Kev disappeared inside the abandoned building and opened the toilet top. He reached inside and grabbed a bundle of dope stamped poison. As soon as Lil Kev stepped outside the building, he saw Twin closely analyzing the money Snaggs gave him. Lil Kev continued toward the two junkies to serve them the poison, but before Lil Kev could hand Snaggs the dope, Twin had peeped the play. Twin was already in motion. He wasn't a magician or illusionist, but the nine millimeter in his hand appeared as if by magic. No one saw him pull it. "Don't fuckin' move!" Twin barked, aiming the gun at Snaggs and his partner in crime. "Go head. Try to run, and I'm gonna empty this mutherfuckin' clip. Do I make myself clear?"

"What's wrong, homey? What the fuck these two niggers do?" Blob asked.

"They violated me. They tried to cop with counterfeit money," Twin proclaimed.

"Oh yeah? Keep them mutherfuckas right here," Blob barked, walking to his car. He opened the trunk and removed a Louisville Slugger baseball bat. The two dope fiends silently cursed themselves for being sloppy. When they realized what was about to take place, the heavyset, light-skinned addict known as Big Red was the first to cop a plea.

"I tried to tell this fool not to try that shit, but he wouldn't listen," said Red to no one in particular. No sooner than he finished his sentence, Blob swung the bat, instantly breaking Red's kneecap. The sound was similar to a major league baseball being smacked out of the stadium.

Red buckled and collapsed to the ground. Snaggs panicked. He ran blindly into the street, screaming for someon.e, anyone, to help. He didn't see the U-Haul truck until it was bearing down on him. By then it was too late. His body collided with the truck and was propelled fifteen feet in the sir. Snaggs landed on his head, fracturing his skull. The burden of carrying an insatiable gorilla on his back for so many years was finally over. Snaggs took his last breath and surrendered his soul to the Grim Reaper.

"Yo, that was some crazy shit," Cee Allah mumbled.

"Fool motherfucka," Zulu snapped.

"Yo, Lil Kev, grab the stash and go home. I'll pick you up tomorrow. Bounce before the five-o rear their ugly heads. Wait, hold up a minute," Twin barked. "That nigga ain't getting off that easy. I'm gonna make an example outta his ass."

Twin pointed the gun at Big Red's ass, and without hesitation he pulled the trigger. The sound of Twin's cannon going off made Lil Kev's ears ring. Big Red started screaming and pleading for his life

"Please, God. Don't kill me," Red cried.

Blob was sitting behind the steering wheel looking through the rearview mirror at Twin as he dumped on Red. He started the car and banged on the horn. When Twin looked in his direction, Blob motioned for them to come the fuck on.

Twin, Cee Allah, and Zulu ran to the car and jumped in. Blob started pressing on the accelerator before the doors were even completely closed.

Lil Kev retrieved the rest of their package and started walking home. On his way home, he couldn't help but replay the scene in his head. No matter how hard Lil Kev tried, he couldn't repress the images of Red getting shot or Snaggs's broken body flying through the air. His young mind was overwhelmed by the brutal consequences the two dope fiends suffered from their underhanded antics. When Lil Kev made it home, he went directly to his bedroom and locked himself in. He removed the fourteen bundles of heroin from his jacket pocket, sat down on the edge of the bed, and stared at the dope as if seeing it for the first time. He couldn't explain or understand it. Nevertheless he sensed the awesome power and subtle wickedness exuding from the substance he held inside his hand.

Kev knew the heroin was partly responsible for Snaggs's death and countless others. He vowed to never use the drug he sold. Suddenly he recalled a significant memory. One morning Twin was taking him to breakfast when they saw a young dope fiend Twin remembered from elementary school. The fiend was in a vacant lot, bent over and throwing up his guts. He was obviously dope sick. "Lil Kev," Twin said after spotting the young fiend from back in the days, "if it wasn't for niggas like that, you and I would just be average mutherfuckas. Our product is all we have in common with them niggas, though.

That's how we coexist. We depend on each other sort of like a pimp depends on his hoes. They're slaves, and we're slave masters. It's of paramount importance you never forget," Twin said, holding up a bundle of dope, "this shit right here is to be sold, not used."

A knock on the door broke Lil Kev's train of thought. "Who is it?" Kevin asked, sliding the dope underneath his bed.

"It's Deyla. Grandma said come eat."

"I'm not hungry," Kevin replied. He picked a tape out of his small collection, inserted it into his Walkman, and pressed play. He lay back on his bed and listened as Rakim Allah's supreme lyrics emitted through the speakers until he dozed off.

The next morning he reluctantly got out of bed and got dressed for school. Kevin quickly ate a bowl of Frosted Flakes and left for school, completely oblivious to the dope he'd carelessly left under the bed.

CHAPTER 8

At 1:30 p.m. Mr. Charlie was approaching his fourth glass of corn liquor. He'd only intended to have a quick taste or two and relax until the Chicago Bulls played the New York Knicks. Then he figured he would have himself a real drink.

Charlie was seated in his personal chair in front of the TV with a glass of corn liquor glued to his lips when Lillian walked into the front room carrying his dinner. "Charlie," she screamed, "put that damn liquor down, and put some food in your stomach. It's too early to be drinking that shit. School hasn't even let out yet, and you're half-drunk already." Lillian frowned, handing her husband a plate of fried chicken, collard greens, and potato salad.

"Please, woman. Don't start no shit, and there won't be none. I only had a little taste," Charlie grunted.

"A little taste my ass, Charlie. You ain't capable of a little taste. You drink like you got gills." Lillian grabbed the jug of corn liquor from behind Charlie's chair, and she yanked the glass from his hand, spilling liquor on the crotch of his pants.

"What's the matter with you, woman?" Charlie shouted, wiping the wet crotch of his pants with the palm of his hand. "Maybe, just maybe, if you stop making that shit so goddamn good, I might give some thought to leaving it alone."

Charlie continued to ramble as his wife exited the room. Lillian had a few hours to spare before school let out, and she had to go back to work to make sure the kids she was responsible for made it safely across the streets. She used the spare time to tidy up the house. When she opened the door to her grandson's room, she was not surprised at its condition. "Just as I expected, this boy's room is a mess," Lillian thought. She didn't have this problem with Libby and Deyla, who shared the same room. They were much more orderly than their brother. Lillian stepped inside the pigpen and immediately began picking clothes up off the floor.

Medina read the note Lil Kev dropped on her desk on his way to the bathroom. A smile developed as she reread the note. "When are you gonna stop teasing a nigga and let me tap that ass?" the note read. Medina looked like the cat who ate the canary. She read the note for a third time and thought, "Shit.

I wish his fine ass could tap it right now in front of the whole classroom."

Both of their desks were situated so they faced each other. Medina knew Lil Kev had been looking between her legs, because she allowed him the opportunity to look. She liked bad boys, and she'd witnessed Lil Kev hugging the block on several occasions with known drug dealers. When Lil Kev returned and sat at his desk, he was greeted with open legs.

He smiled openly at the lovely sight, and he became aroused at how her pink flower cotton panties seemed to be choking the life out of her crotch. Kev drifted back to his very first sexual encounter. He'd just joined Twin's team and finished his first package when Twin decided to show him how much he appreciated Lil Kev's help. Twin had one of his freaks reward Lil Kev with his first blow job and orgasm that wasn't self-induced.

Lil Kev looked up to Twin like the big brother he never had. He dug Twin for more reasons than one. Most of all he dug him because Twin treated Kevin and the rest of his team with respect and not like the fifteen-year-old he was. Suddenly he remembered who was picking him up after school. "Oh shit," he blurted while checking his pockets. "

In addition to his broken leg, Big Red had also gotten hit with a hot slug from Twin's nine milly before they fled the scene. It was only a flesh wound, which wasn't half as serious as his partner's predicament. He would survive; Snaggs wasn't as fortunate. Big Red surfed the channels with the remote control attached to his bed until he came across an episode of *Saturday Night Live*. He lay on his side recovering from a broken kneecap and a gunshot wound to his right ass cheek at Cook County Hospital.

Red had absolutely no way of knowing he and Snaggs would end up facing such disastrous consequences for copping dope with counterfeit money. It was something they did regularly. Red had entertained the thought of kicking the habit numerous times, but it was always a fleeting thought. Now, lying in his hospital bed, he was seriously considering it.

He wanted to starve the gorilla on his back to death. Someone had called an ambulance, and when the ambulance arrived, Snaggs was pronounced DOA. His body was shipped to the county morgue while the doctors at Cook County Hospital put Red's broken leg in a cast and attended to his gunshot wound. They had also called the cops and informed them of Red's gunshot wound, which was standard procedure for doctors.

When Big Red was questioned by the cops, he told them he was trying to buy some dope to get off, and he got caught in a cross fire instead. When they questioned him about Snaggs, Red said he was solo and denied ever knowing him.

"This boy's room is filthy," Lillian thought as she swept the floor in Lil Kev's bedroom. She swept under his bed where the majority of dust had accumulated. She stared at she swept from under the bed. Puzzled at what she saw, Lillian bent down to get a closer look. She began to comprehend what she was staring at. She couldn't believe what was on the floor in her grandson's bedroom. Her eyes teared up, making her vision blurry. Her facial expression changed from astonishment to pain to pure rage within a matter of seconds. Using the tips of her fingers only, Lillian carefully picked up the ziplock bag containing the bundles of heroin from the floor. She carried the package to the bathroom, holding it with her fingertips as if carrying a bag of shit. Lillian lifted the lid of the toilet and began dropping bundles of heroin inside the commode. One of the bundles bounced off the rim of the seat and landed on the floor. Lillian picked it up and read the stamp on one of the bags. It said poison.

"That's exactly what this shit is. Poison," Lillian mumbled as she dropped the bundle of dope in the commode with the rest and flushed the toilet. She was so upset she almost forgot she had to go back to work. Fortunately the job was right across the street from Lillian's house. She put on her crossing guard jacket and walked out the door thinking about the best solution to solving this problem with her grandson.

CHAPTER 9

Renee could've easily been selected as the poster girl for the fountain of youth. She was thirtyish but didn't look a day over twenty-five. Renee was blessed with natural yet raw beauty. It was the kind of beauty that didn't require makeup. Her complexion was flawless. Every player, old or young, who encountered her thirsted to drink from her fountain. Of course, their paper had to be long enough to get a sip.

Posing naked in front of her huge bedroom mirror, Renee twisted and turned, inspecting her curvy frame with the attitude of a true Narcissus. She ran her finger lightly across the flat surface of her abdomen and then cupped both tits in the palms of her hands. She juggled them up and down like water balloons. She lifted one up to her mouth and flicked her tongue across the nipple until it became hard. Then she repeated the act with her right tit. Renee switched back and forth until both nipples stood at attention. Her phone rang inside her bedroom, interrupting her erotic solo act. "Damn," Renee exclaimed aloud, reluctantly giving both nipples a farewell kiss.

On the fourth ring of the phone, Renee snatched the phone off its cradle and shouted, "Who's this?"

"It's your mother. Is that how you answer the phone, Renee? What the hell is the matter with you?"

"I'm sorry, Mama. It's that time of the month," Renee lied.

"I need you to come get your son immediately. He can't stay in my house anymore."

"Why? What's wrong, Mama?"

"I'll explain when you get here. Just hurry up," Lillian replied, hanging up the phone.

When Renee arrived at her mother's apartment, Lillian spotted her from the window getting out of her car. Lillian opened the door before Renee knocked. Renee kissed her mother on the cheek as she entered the apartment.

"What did he do this time, Mama?"

"Don't come in my house questioning me. You don't have no patience at all," Lillian huffed.

"Where's my son at?" Renee asked.

"He better be in that goddamn room," Lillian snapped. "I was sweeping the floor in his room and found a sandwich bag full of some shit called poison."

"What are you talking about? Some shit called poison? I don't understand."

"Dope. Heroin. A big ass sandwich bag of that shit with the name poison stamped on each bag. Kevin had that shit inside my house."

"Mama, my son don't use drugs." It was all Renee could say.

"Did I say he was using drugs? I said I found a bag of that shit under his bed. He's selling that shit."

"Where did he get it from?"

"You know how much I love that boy, but I tried to beat the life outta him, and he still wouldn't tell me the truth. The good Lord knows it's bad enough I sell liquor to make ends meet, but I refuse to allow my grandson, or anybody else, to bring drugs in my house." Lillian turned her back on Renee and started toward her bedroom.

"What did you do with the drugs?" Renee asked, following her mother into her bedroom.

"What do you think I did with it, Renee? I flushed it down the toilet. That's what I did with it. God knows I love that boy to death, but I gotta draw the line somewhere. His clothes are already packed."

"Kevin," Renee shouted, "let's go. Now!"

Kevin came out of his bedroom carrying his suitcase with his head hung low. Renee stared at her son then shook her head. "Bye, Grandma," Kevin mumbled on his way out the door.

"Kevin, whatever you done got involved in, I want you to stop it, you hear me, boy?"

"Yes," Kevin muttered.

"Yes what?"

"Yes, Mom."

Kevin loved his grandmother, and he knew she loved him. He also knew he fucked up big time, and it would take some time before she forgave him. He opened the door to Renee's new Corvette, put his suitcase on the backseat, and leaped into the car, closing the door behind him. Renee started the car, checked the rearview mirror, and eased out into traffic. She made a right turn at the corner of Forty-seventh and King Drive, and she drove down the congested street toward Michigan Ave. before speaking. "Kevin, where did you get that dope from? Before you answer me, though, if you don't trust me enough to be honest, I prefer you not say nothing at all."

Kevin stared out the window as they cruised past all the different establishments. Renee stopped at a red light and glanced over at her son. "Did you hear what I asked you?"

"Yeah, Renee. I heard you."

"Then answer me. Where did you get that shit from?"

"I took it. I saw a dude stash it behind the wheel of an abandoned car. When he wasn't paying attention, I took it."

"Why would you take somebody's package? What was you gonna do with it?" asked Renee.

"I told you the truth. I took it," Kevin responded, still looking out the window. "I was gonna give it to my people to sell for me."

"Kevin, you need to concentrate on school and your future. Not on drugs or anybody associated with that shit. Do you wanna end up dead like your father or in jail for life like your cousin, Mo? Either way you lose. Ain't no future in that shit."

They approached the intersection at Forty-seventh and Michigan Avenue. Renee turned left and took Michigan Avenue all the way up to Sixty-ninth Street, where she lived in a two-bedroom apartment she rented after Lillian decided to raise her children.

Renee stopped at another red light on Fifty-first and Michigan, and she noticed how Kevin twisted around in his seat. He was following the movement of a husky young man walking an American pit bull terrier with a huge tow truck chain around the dog's neck. When Blob recognized Lil Kev, he yanked the chain, stopping the dog abruptly in its tracks. He acknowledged Lil Kev with a head nod, which didn't escape Renee's vision. Renee pressed down on the accelerator when the light turned green, and then she turned on the radio. "Who was the boy, Kevin? And why was he looking as if he wanted to say something to you?"

"That was Blob. He hustles around Grandma's house," Kevin responded. As Renee thought about what her son just said, she became skeptical of his story about how he came into possession of the drugs. Renee made a mental note to start paying close attention to the company her son kept. When they made it home, Renee went straight to her bedroom and pressed play on her answering machine. She had two messages, and she listened to them both. The first message said, "Hi. It's Mimi. Girl, I'm definitely missing you. What have I done to deserve this kind of treatment? Call me." Beep.

The second message started. The voice was only a whisper. "Renee, it's Mimi again. Listen, I got something really special for you, and I'm bursting at the seams to see how it looks on you. Please call me. I'm waiting." Beep.

Renee made a mental note to return Mimi's call, and then she went into the kitchen to make cheeseburgers and French fries for dinner. Kevin got himself situated in his new bedroom. When he finished unpacking and putting away his belongings, he picked up the phone in the bedroom to page Twin. Two minutes later the phone rang. "I got it, Renee," Kevin yelled, snatching the phone off its cradle.

"Who this?" Twin barked into the phone.

"It's Lil Kev. What's up, Twin?"

"What's up yourself, nigga? I came to scoop you behind the school today so we can get this paper, but you was missing in action. Nigga, I waited for a half hour parked in that fuckin' alley with a pistol in my car. I felt like a mutherfuckin' sitting duck, Kevin." The only time Twin called him Kevin was when he was upset with him, and Lil Kev was fully aware of that. "Why the fuck didn't you wait for me?" Twin snapped. Before Kev could respond, Twin asked, "Where the fuck you at?"

"I'm at Renee's crib. My grandmother kicked me out her house today and shit."

"What?" Twin uttered in surprise. "For what?"

"She found my stash," Kev whispered.

"How the fuck you let that happen? You slipping, nigga!"

"Nah, Twin, I swear it ain't like that. I had it stashed under my bed, and she decided to clean my room while I was at school, and she stumbled across it. We wouldn't be going through this shit if I didn't have to go to school. I hate school. I could be out there with y'all getting money. That school shit is for suckers," Lil Kev exclaimed.

"You finished talking yet?" Twin snapped. "Boy, you sound like a sucka. If you quit school, I'm gonna quit you. I'm gonna cut you off. I'm dead serious, nigga."

"Kevin, who are you talking to on my phone?" Renee shouted.

"Hold on, Twin. It's my folks, Renee!" yelled Kevin.

"How the hell did your folks know to call you here, Kevin?"

"Because I paged him! Kevin yelled back

Twin, I'm sorry, man. I'll work it off, OK?"

"Don't be sorry, Lil Kev. Shit happens. Just be more careful. I'm gonna pick you up after school tomorrow. If I'm not there when you get out, wait for me. You know you gotta get down and dirty, right?"

"Yeah, folks. I know. I'll see you tomorrow." Kev hung up the phone.

"Wash your hands," Renee said as Lil Kev exited his room. At the kitchen table Renee asked her son for his folks' names. "Which one of my folks?" Lil Kev responded.

"Don't get cute, nigga. The one you just finished talking to on my phone."

"Oh, his name's Twin."

"Kevin, why do Twin need a pager? Does he sell drugs?"

"I don't know, Renee. Why don't you ask him?"

"Because I'm asking you, boy, but if he calls here again, best believe I'm gonna do just that. Oh, and one more thing, do not bring none of that shit in this house 'cause if you do, you'll be homeless. You've been forewarned."

When they finished eating, Lil Kev went to his room, turned on the TV, and lay across his bed thinking about his sisters and if his grandmother would ever let him live in her house again.

Renee washed the dishes and then returned Mimi's call. "You mentioned you had something very special for me. I'm curious. What can that special something be?" Renee asked.

"It's something I know you're gonna love, but I'm not telling you what it is over the phone. When can you come find out what I got for you?"

CHAPTER 10

"Shake it, Son of a Bitch! Shake it out," Blob shouted, and the dog responded. The pit bull held the opposite end of the hemp rope, shaking and pulling it with tremendous physical force. Both of the dog's front paws were planted deeply in Blob's midsection for maximum leverage as it attempted to rip the rope to shreds, nearly dislocating Blob's shoulder blade in the process.

"*Oust*," Blob yelled, which was a German command he taught the dog meaning "stop." Reluctantly the dog stopped shaking the rope, but he refused to release it. After prying the rope out of Son of a Bitch's mouth, the dog received a full body rubdown, some fresh water, and some much-needed dog rest. Son of a Bitch was a well conditioned pit bull. He weighed forty-eight pounds. His coat was sable, his eyes were pinkish, and he had a red nose. On the chain, Son of a Bitch was fifty-five pounds with a huge bucket head. Also he was an extremely hard biter. Son of a Bitch was sired by Chatman's bone head, out of Hunts Point Gold digger. He was a three-year-old grand champion pit bull terrier.

Blob had been training Son of a Bitch for three months for the up-and-coming match, which had finally arrived. Today was the day of the scheduled match. Beside Son of a Bitch, Blob owned four more pit bulls. There were three bitches (dams) and one male (sire). Son of a Bitch was Blob's prize possession, however, and he was the only champion he had that ever wore a collar. All his dogs were fighters, but not all of them were game. Two of his bitches, Tramp and Lou Lou, were both game dogs, but the other bitch, Cleo, and the other male, Leather Face, were suspect. However, Son of a Bitch was the closest to dead game as any living dog could be. He had stopped a total of seven dogs in his career. Three of those died inside the pit in less than forty minutes. One dog turned after a hard bite to the chest, and one wouldn't scratch after absorbing twenty-three minutes of pure punishment. His last two opponents jumped the pit. One was able to escape, but the other got caught by the stifle and drug back into the pit. He was mangled until his handler was forced to pick him up.

After today's match Blob intended on retiring Son of a Bitch and breeding him with Tramp. Tramp was a forty-pound tiger striped bitch he purchased eighteen months ago from Crowbar Kennel. Tramp was Blob's favorite bitch. She had two wins. Her first win was over a thirty-eight pound white bitch named Slave. She stopped Slave in one hour and ten minutes. Her second win was over a forty-two-pound bitch named Black Widow, who she stopped in one hour and twenty-two minutes. Tramp definitely had potential. Blob didn't believe in breeding curs, which are dogs that stop fighting before the match is over.

This led Blob to believe that Tramp and Son of a Bitch could produce a litter with a few game pups. Once Son of a Bitch was back inside the kennel, Blob paged Twin and informed him of the scheduled event. Twin loved dogfighting almost as much as Blob loved pit bulls. Twin was lounging inside his late model BMW, chewing on a cheese hoagie and observing the scenery while his crew openly pitched dope on the block as if they had licenses to do so. Twin watched as the green Malibu crept slowly up the block toward his car and then stopped next to him.

When Twin recognized the driver, he released the grip on his gun and lowered the window. "What's up, Pimp?"

Pimp was once a rising star in the circle of pimps and hoes. When a hoe chose him, the first thing Pimp would do is poison her and then charge her for the cure. Pimp once controlled as many as eight hoes, until he started sniffing dope and eventually caught a habit. The habit progressed until it spiraled out of control and robbed Pimp of his ambition. The constant use of heroin reduced Pimp from an up-and-coming hoe handler to a pitiful relic of the past. He was driven by desperation to satisfy an insatiable gorilla. Pimp currently had two prostitutes, and both were dope fiends. They were a salt and pepper team. His bottom bitch was named Pepper. She was black. Salt was his Anglo-Saxon white hoe. Pepper was there when Pimp was on the rise, and she stayed with him after his fall.

"Ain't nothin' to me but what you see," Pimp responded. "I heard you got some shit called poison that's jumping up and down, screaming, and hollering."

"Yeah, that's right. On a scale of one to ten, it's an eight and a half. It's definitely something to write home about," replied Twin.

"In that case I better grab two bundles," said Pimp, handing $160 to Pepper, who was in the backseat. "Here, bitch, get two bundles." Pepper took the money from Pimp's hand and began to count it. "Bitch, what the fuck are you doing? It's all there. Since you counting, count it fair. If you count it crooked, I'm gonna think you took it. Now get your punk ass out of this pimpmobile and cop the dope before they run out," Pimp screamed.

Twin was about to tell Pimp not to worry and that he had plenty of dope when his pager started vibrating. He took the pager off his hip and checked the number. Twin recognized the code 357 immediately. Blob had chosen the code 357 because it was the weapon he preferred to carry. Twin opened the door and stepped out of the car. He walked the short distance to the pay phone on the corner. He picked up the receiver, dropped a quarter into the slot, and proceeded to dial the number on his pager.

Before the first ring was complete, Blob snatched the receiver off the hook. "What up, Twin?" he barked.

"I'm good. What's up with you folks?"

"Today is the day, baby," Blob said excitedly.

"Today is the day for what? You getting married or something and just decided to tell me?" Twin chuckled.

"Hell nah, nigga. It's even better than that. Son of a Bitch has got a match in two hours."

"For real? Where at?" asked Twin.

"On Fortieth and State in the projects," said Blob.

"There are a lot of projects on Fortieth and State. Which building, nigga?"

"Building 4022 on the fourteenth floor in 1406."

"Whose apartment is that?"

"Nobody's. It's abandoned," said Blob. "Twin, I'm telling you, man. You can bet yo whole stash. Even the safe at yo mama's house. Jewelry and all. Son of a Bitch is gonna mangle his opponent."

"Blob, as much as I wanna believe you, convince me why I should. Every nigga I know that fucks with pit bulls says the same shit about his dogs. He says how game this bitch is or how hard this one bites."

"Now, folks, have I ever lied to you? I was raised with dogs."

"Who's Son of a Bitch matched up with?" Twin asked.

"He's fighting this forty-eight pound black and white pit bull named Bottom Line. I've never heard of that dog before, but I don't give a fat baby's blue, rashy ass who he is matched with. This mutherfucka is unstoppable. I've had over thirty dogs in my life, Twin, but nothin' I ever had compares to Son of a Bitch. Feel me? After he wins today's match, I'm gonna retire my champion and breed him."

"Breed him with who? Tramp?" Twin asked.

"Hell nah. I'm gonna get one of those crackhead chicks off the block and pay her to come to the kennel so my dog can get a royal treat. You feel me? The nigga deserves it."

"Blob, you can't be serious," Twin chuckled.

"I play a lot of games, but when it concerns my dogs, my pride and joy dogs, I'm more serious than a plane crash."

"All right, nigga, you convinced me. I'll be there. I got twenty-five hundred on Son of a Bitch." Twin smiled, knowing Blob appreciated his confidence in Son of a Bitch.

"Yeah, that's what I wanna hear. Guess what, nigga?"

"I'm not good at guessing. Just tell me what it is," Twin said.

"OK, listen. If Son of a Bitch loses the match, which is highly unlikely, I'll refund half your money. That's how confident I am in my dog," Blob barked.

"All right, folks, I'll see you at the match then." Twin hung up the phone. On the way back to his car, Twin motioned to Zulu to join him.

"What's up, Twin?" Zulu said in his deep, baritone voice as he reached the car.

"Ain't nothing. Listen, I want y'all to grind hard for one more hour, shut down, and meet me on the block."

"It's only a quarter to five right now," said Zulu. "So at six o'clock, it's a wrap. That's what you telling me?"

"Exactly, and then I want y'all to wait for me on the block."

Twin raced to his mother's house on Ninety-first and Bennet. When Twin arrived on his mother's block, he parked, got out, and proceeded up the front stairs. He used the key she gave him nine years earlier, when he was still in middle school. He loved his mother and would visit her at every opportunity. He closed the door and rushed down the stairs to the basement where his safe was located. Twin slid the connecting washer and dryer away from the wall and started aligning the sequence of numbers on the combination lock until the safe opened.

Instead of removing the cash by individual stacks, he stuck his whole arm inside the safe and scooped all the money onto the basement floor. The money was wrapped in rubber bands in thousand-dollar stacks. When Twin finished counting, there were seventy-four stacks. Twin picked up three stacks and tossed the rest back into the safe, locked it, and stuffed the three grand into his pocket. He slid the washer and dryer back in place and went back upstairs to the kitchen.

Twin opened the refrigerator, grabbed a chicken wing out of a Tupperware bowl, and demolished it cold. Twin then took a pen that was attached to a magnet on the refrigerator and wrote a note to his mother. "Your Twin was here. I wish you was home so we could've had lunch together. How about this weekend? I'll call you later. Love, Twin." Maurice, which was

Twin's given name, was a twin. However, his twin brother died during birth from complications. Before he made his exit, Twin couldn't resist the urge to help himself to another piece of his mother's delicious fried chicken.

Twin left the house and locked the front door behind him. Still munching on the chicken, he got back in his car and headed back toward the low end to pick up his crew and take them to the dog match to see the champion Son of a Bitch do what he did best—mangle.

Renee's sleep was interrupted by the sound of her alarm clock. She had totally forgotten she'd even set it until she suddenly remembered why. Kevin. "I gotta get him up for school," she thought while shutting off the alarm. The time was 6:45 a.m. Renee got out of bed and went to the bathroom to pee. When she finished, she proceeded to Kevin's bedroom, only to find it empty. "Kevin! Boy, where are you?" Renee shouted as she walked toward the kitchen.

"I'm in the kitchen," Kevin yelled.

When Renee reached the kitchen, she was surprised to see her son fully dressed and eating a bowl of cereal. "Good morning, handsome."

"'Sup, Renee?" Lil Kev replied.

"How long you been awake?"

"About an hour. Why?"

"Just curious. What's wrong? You didn't sleep well?"

"Ain't nothin' wrong. I'm just used to getting up early. The early bird gets the worm." Kevin smirked, shoving a spoonful of Captain Crunch into his mouth.

Renee stared at him while he chewed on the cereal. Her hands were on her hips. She shook her head with a pensive expression plastered on her face. "Who told you that bullshit?" she asked.

"Twin, my homey," Lil Kev murmured.

"Well, the next time Twin tells you about the party, make sure he tells you about the picnic too," said Renee. She was standing in the middle of the kitchen floor in her nightgown with her hands still glued to her curvy hips. She was anticipating a response from her son.

The response didn't come right away. Instead Kevin just eyeballed his narcissistic mother. He was thinking how beautiful she was, even in the morning. Lil Kev wanted his wife to possess the same beauty. "What picnic you talking about, Renee?" he finally asked.

"Baby," Renee began, using her hands to emphasize her point. "The early bird doesn't always get the worm. Sometimes the bird gets eaten by the snake." Renee walked out of the kitchen. She got dressed so she could drop Kevin off at school. Kevin finished eating his breakfast and tried to make sense out of what Renee meant.

Lil Kev was behind his school waiting for fifteen minutes before Twin rolled up. "Get in the car, folks," Twin snapped.

Lil Kev opened the car door and tossed his book bag on the backseat. He sat down in the passenger seat and closed the door. "What's up, little nigga? You ready to get this money?"

"Hell yeah," responded Lil Kev. "That's like asking a blind mutherfucka do he wanna see."

Twin smiled and reached underneath the seat to retrieve a large sandwich bag of bundles stamped poison. He tossed them in Lil Kev's lap. "Your vision is in that bag. Tell me what you see," Twin said, slowly pulling off.

"I see greenbacks, mutherfucka. What else?" Lil Kev chuckled.

"Good. Now listen, as soon as you finish that work, I'm gonna squash your debt, all right?"

"Yeah, all right," Lil Kev responded.

"I got you, little nigga. I'm not gonna leave you fucked up."

"I'm not gonna leave you fucked up either," Lil Kev countered. "Watch, I'm gonna finish this shit like clockwork," said Kev, tossing the heavy sandwich bag in his hands. "You ever seen Clark Kent turn into Superman?"

"Yeah. Why?" Twin asked, turning toward Lil Kev.

"Cause that's how fast I'm gonna get rid of this shit." Lil Kev smirked.

"That's why I fuck with you, nigga. 'Cause you know how to get at a dollar," Twin chuckled.

"You ain't gotta gas me up. I'm gonna take care of my bitch regardless," said Lil Kev, stuffing the sandwich bag of dope down the front of his pants.

"Handle yo business then, lil nigga," Twin barked.

Forty-seventh and Michigan Avenue was a honey hole. It was also the block and headquarters where poison was sold. It was the block Twin and his crew had in a choke hold. It was off-limits to sell product there if you weren't part of Twin's team. Twin wouldn't have it and neither would his trigger-happy enforcers, Sincere and Blob. Both had a propensity for violence. Twin had already been tried and tested in the past by rival gangs and drug dealers, who had learned the hard way the poison crew was nobody to take lightly.

They were willing to do whatever it took to maintain what it had taken years to build. However, Twin preferred going to war as a last result because of the heat it bought. His enforcers, Blob and Sincere, had résumés so lengthy that had they chosen legal professions, promotions would've been first priority. Zulu's job was to cut and package the product and make sure the profit made it to the stash house. This was six blocks away from where they operated. Black Sun, Cee Allah, Lil Kev, and Blaze (Pitchers) all rode to the stash house with Zulu in his Cherokee Jeep to drop the money.

As instructed, they returned to the block to wait for Twin's arrival. When they returned to the block, dope fiends were marching around like ants. They had gotten the word that poison closed early and would remain closed for the remainder of the day. In a panicked frenzy, they came together to brainstorm about where they could cop the next best bag.

At approximately 6:15 p.m., the crew spotted their partner and boss rolling slowly up the block. They were piled inside Zulu's Jeep smoking weed and politicking about which bitch gave the best head. Black Sun was bragging about how he got sucked off by two neighborhood cockologists. "Folks, check it out, right. I climbed on the hood of a motherfuckin' Ford station wagon that was parked in the vacant lot on the side of the Chinese cleaners. I'm posted up with my arms crossed while Vanessa's tall, lanky ass stood on the ground in front of me. She was holding my ankles so I couldn't move while she ate me alive. I was buried to the hilt in that long ass neck of hers with my balls on her chin. That shit was spooky 'cause I was pounding her throat with every inch of this African soup bone, and this giraffe didn't even gag, but she don't got shit on Connie."

Connie was a self-proclaimed technician in the art of fellatio. She'd developed her own unique style and named it brainstorm. Everybody that got the chance to sample Connie's technique had one thing in common. They were extremely satisfied. Connie was in a class by herself. She was coined the headhunter. "Also that yellow bitch is dead gorgeous," Black Sun continued. "That petite bitch surprised me. I underestimated her. Until that encounter, I ain't never had a bitch make me lose consciousness. At one point it felt like she was trying to suck the enamel off my dick. Ke ke ke. I was done on both sides."

"Nigga, dicks ain't made outta enamel. Teeth is," Cee Allah interjected.

"I'm just saying, that bitch had me so open, she could've played me. Pretended like she was gonna stop, and I would've gave her every motherfuckin' dime in my pocket, including this Cuban link on my neck. The head was superb. When it was over, I felt like the bitch stuck me up. That's how incredible that shit felt, and check it out, I been chasing that feeling ever since."

"Damn, where the bitch live at? I want a sample," said Cee Allah. Black Sun laughed. "What the fuck is you laughing for? I'm serious, nigga," Cee Allah snapped.

"I know that bitch you talking about," said Sincere. "I bumped into her one night coming outta Jerry's spot, and—"

"For real?" Zulu asked.

"Nah, for play. Shut the fuck up and listen. As I was saying, I spotted her leaving Jerry's after-hours joint, and I kidnapped that hazel-eyed bitch. I took her to the Roberts Motel, you know what I'm saying? I got her high and made her beg me to put my gun in her mouth. Feel me? Then I went swimming in that tight little pussy," Sincere proclaimed with an arrogant smirk.

"For real, though," said Black Sun, "didn't she try to swallow your whole dick?"

Sincere looked at Black Sun as if he'd been caught smoking crack. "Freak ass nigga, I'm not talking about the gun in my pants. I put my actual pistol in her mouth."

Everybody inside the Jeep exploded in laughter except Lil Kev. He didn't see the humor. Before Twin could finish parking his car, his crew exited the Jeep and stood on the sidewalk, waiting for him to get out of the car. When Twin stepped out of his car, he gave everybody a pound. "What's up, y'all? Everything aiight?"

Zulu was the first to respond. "Yeah, everything is peaches and cream. What's up with you? You got us shutting down early with all this money still out here. What's the science with that?"

"No need for greed. Tomorrow's another day. As soon as we start getting greedy, the next thing you know, envy and jealousy will come into play and consume us. Once that happens, we're finished. Anything that can happen will happen. Greed kills more niggas than bullets. You just continue to make sure our product stays above average, and let me worry about how and when we get this paper.

"Sincere, you and Lil Kev can ride with me. The rest of y'all can follow in the Jeep. We going to the projects on Fortieth Street."

Once they were inside Twin's car, Lil Kev handed Twin two knots of money and said, "I told you I was gonna finish that package with swiftness."

"Is this the whole thing?" asked Twin.

"Yeah! That's sixteen hundred bucks," said Lil Kev.

Twin peeled off three hundred dollars and passed it to Lil Kev. "Didn't I tell you I wasn't gonna leave you fucked up?"

Renee stood on top of Mimi's chrome and mahogany dresser inside Mimi's bedroom. She was posing with a joint in her mouth. She was scantily clad. Eighty percent of her body was exposed, and twenty percent was covered by a red and black bra and matching G-string, which had disappeared between the cleft of her incredible behind. Renee rotated her hips in a circular motion to the tune of "Private Dancer" by Tina Turner as it bellowed from the speakers.

She had actually lost count of how many times she had indulged in consensual sex with Mimi since that first episode, which was over five years ago. The more she reflected on the unfolding perversion inside Mimi's bedroom, the stronger her reserve became. Her facial expression was pensive, and her eyes were dreamy looking. The clarity of her behavior caused a mood swing, which affected her performance. What Renee didn't understand was that everybody has a self-accusing spirit inside.

This accusatory spirit is activated when one crosses the line from morality to immorality. It can't be seen with the naked eye or touched, but it can definitely be felt. It's that internal voice audible to the mind only, and it is consciously connected to the principle of right and wrong, good and bad, and positive and negative. Imagine having a built-in alarm that goes off inside the brain when one deviates from a refined perspective in thought, deed, or action. That's what the self-accusing spirit is equivalent to. Renee's spirit was pointing at her and accusing her of awful things. She felt her soul was on trial, and her spirit was the star witness testifying against her.

The verdict was guilty. She was emotionally convicted of conspiring with her body to commit uninhibited sexual acts for monetary and material profit. She was also guilty of child neglect and abandonment in the first degree. For the first time in Renee's life, she felt morally dirty.

"What's the matter with you, Renee?" Mimi asked, concerned with Renee's sudden mood swing.

"What's the matter?" Renee thought. "A lot is the matter. I feel like a fuckin' freak of nature. Multiply that by the fact I feel like an unfit mother, and it can be deduced why I'm so unhappy."

The overwhelming feeling of despondency forced Renee to question her integrity. "Ain't nothing the matter. I was just thinking how considerate it was of you to give me this sexy lingerie set," Renee lied, forcing a smile.

She disrobed completely. She stepped down from the dresser and made her way toward the bed where Mimi was lying. Renee climbed on the bed and sat down on top of Mimi's stomach. Lowering her face toward Mimi, she whispered, "I got something special for you too."

"Oh yeah? Then let me have it," Mimi purred.

Renee showered Mimi's entire face with small kisses before sticking her long tongue inside Mimi's mouth. Mimi sucked on the tongue as if it was a small cock.

Twin knocked on the door of apartment 1406. Within seconds a male's voice on the other side shouted, "Yeah? Who is it?"

"It's Twin."

Blob's youngest brother, Logic, opened the door and stepped aside so Twin and his crew could enter the abandoned apartment. Two matches were scheduled for the evening. The first match, which involved two bitches, was already in session when the poison crew made their way to the back of the apartment where the pit was set up. As soon as Blob saw Twin, his whole demeanor changed. Twin's presence caused a metamorphosis in Blob's black, chubby face. His infamous aggressive bully persona melted. His eyes brightened. The corners of his mouth curved upward, forming a huge Kool-Aid smile. He rushed over to where Twin was standing and gave him a bear hug. "I'm glad you showed up. You know how much this shit means to me," Blob whispered in Twin's ear.

"Yeah, folks, I know. I'm gonna drop twenty-five hundred bucks, so it means a lot to me too. Where's the champ? I wanna see Billy Bad Ass."

"Come with me. He's in the bathroom. Twin, this fight's gonna be a cakewalk. It'll be the easiest grand I ever made. Trust me," Blob smiled.

"Who he fighting? Bottoms Up? What you say his opponent's name is?" Twin asked.

"Bottom Line," Blob corrected.

"Yeah, Bottom Line. You said that Bottom Line likes to fight the legs?" Twin asked.

"That's right. I told you so you could have an idea of his fighting style, but he's still gonna lose. As soon as that bitch mutherfucka go for my champ's legs, he's gonna tuck them mutherfuckers like I taught him to do," Blob said.

When Blob opened the bathroom door, Son of a Bitch leaped up, planting both paws on Blob's chest. Then he started panting and whining. It seemed like the dog knew from past experience that the moment of truth had once again arrived for him to go into the pit. Son of a Bitch was so anxious to get busy he couldn't stop whining.

"Calm the fuck down, boy. You gonna get yo shit off in a few," said Blob, simultaneously rubbing the dog's ribs. Twin was amazed at the conformation of the dog. He was obviously well groomed and conditioned, and he exuded power and confidence. His body was lean with almost 0 percent body fat. His coat looked velvet, and his muscles resembled steel.

"Damn, this dog looks like it was manufactured and put together piece by piece," Twin thought.

"Blob, bring Son of a Bitch outta the shit house. It's show-time," Logic yelled.

Blob grabbed Son of a Bitch by the back of his neck and walked him through the house toward the back room. When they reached the pit, men were exchanging money that had been won or lost from the first match. There were fourteen men in the house. Weed smoke permeated the entire apartment. Forty-ounce bottles littered the floor. Bottom Line was already in his corner. Bottom Line was a black dog with white socks (feet). His left eye was circled in white. His right ear was completely ripped off, and from the top of his diamond-shaped head down to his muzzle, he was perforated with teeth marks. Old scar tissue covered both front legs from previous battles. Bottom Line was heavy. He was two pounds over the required weight for the match, which was forty-eight pounds per dog. When Son of a Bitch entered the pit, Bottom Line went bloodthirsty berserk. He growled, barked, and tried to pull his handler across the pit to get at Son of a Bitch, who wasn't even acting aggressive. After all the bets were placed, the referee shouted, "Face your dogs."

Both handlers, Moose and Blob, pointed the dogs toward each other. Son of a Bitch transformed. He was all business now.

He pulled forward with his ears and tail standing straight up. He was intensely aware of the other dog's presence.

"Release yo dogs," the referee screamed.

Both dogs charged forward, colliding like a Mack truck into a brick wall. Bottom Line stormed Son of a Bitch, driving him into the pit wall with tremendous force. Bottom Line took hold of Son of a Bitch's left ear, brutally shaking it.

He released his hold on the ear and went for his favorite hold, the leg. As soon as Son of a Bitch felt the snout of his opponent on his right leg, he tucked both legs, grabbed the back of Bottom Line's neck, and locked on it. Blob was so excited it was difficult for him to breath. "Shake it out, champ. Shake his fuckin' neck off," Blob screamed. "Twin, did you see that shit? That nigga tucked his legs exactly like I taught him to do in that situation."

Son of a Bitch had Bottom Line in a vise grip hold, and he proceeded to shake so viciously that he ripped open a huge hole in the dog's neck. Blood shot out of Bottom Line's neck like water from a broken faucet. Blood even splattered on the clothes of a few spectators. Bottom Line began to sing, and the more he whined, the more Blob yelled for Son of a Bitch to shake it out.

"Stop the fight!" Moose yelled.

Blob ignored him and continued to shout, "Shake it off. Kill him boy!"

It was clear Son of a Bitch had defeated Bottom Line. Still it wasn't enough for Blob. He wanted his dog to murder his opponent, which was inevitable.

"He's killing my dog. Break it up," Bottom Line's owner screamed.

"Shake it out, champ!" Blob screamed at the top of his voice.

"Blob, that's enough. It's over,"Twin said to his friend.

Unbeknownst to the men in the room, they had ceased to exist. Blob was in a world of his own, where he and the dogs were the only remaining sources of existence. Blob couldn't hear the other men literally pleading with him to get his dog. He was oblivious to the presence of everybody inside the room, including Twin. Bottom Line wasn't singing anymore. He'd stop fighting completely, and his body lay limp.

"Open his ass up, champ. Finish what you started," Blob continued.

A single gunshot rang out. The sound was so deafening it penetrated Blob's conscious mind and yanked him out of his hypnotic trance. Blob stared at his dog lying motionless on the pit floor, still locked on Bottom Line's neck. As the reality of what had just happened dawned on him, an ocean of tears surfaced in his eyes, slightly obscuring his vision. The tears rolled down his cheeks.

The room turned into utter chaos. Black Sun and Sincere had Zeek, the man who shot Blob's dog, in the corner of the room at gunpoint. Moose pulled out a 3.80 and pointed it at Blob's head. "Nigga, I tried to tell yo deaf ass to stop the fight yesterday. Now it's too fuckin' late. You gonna die with yo—"

Before Moose finished his sentence, Twin eased up on him and cracked him in the back of his head with a chrome 45 automatic. Moose collapsed on the floor, losing consciousness. Twin bent over Moose, picked up his gun, and put it inside his waistband. Then Twin quickly rifled through Moose's pants pockets, relieving him of nine hundred dollars in cash.

Blob's tears began to dry, but his expression still reflected the extent of his pain and anger. When Blob finally spoke, his voice was so low it was barely audible. "Which one of these niggas did it?"

"This bitch ass nigga right here," Sincere barked, punching Zeek in his mouth.

Blob pulled the .357 Magnum out of his waistband, cocked it, and said, "Move out the way."

Not wanting to get hit by a stray bullet, Sincere and Black sun quickly stepped aside.

"Please, man. Don't kill me," Zeek cried, reaching into his front pocket. "Here, take this change. That's five thousand dollars. Just don't kill me."

"Lil Kev, get that loot from that dead nigga," Blob barked.

Lil Kev stepped over to Zeek and took the money out of his hand. "Take off that jewelry too. You ain't gonna need it where you going," said Lil Kev. "Nigga, you violated, so take what you got coming, pussy mutherfucka."

Blob stepped forward and squeezed off two shots in rapid succession. The first slug hit Zeek in his chest. The second one kissed him on the mouth and exited through the back of his skull. Zeek's very last thought was, "How can these rotten bastards take my life in exchange for a fuckin' dog?"

Zeek perished on his feet. The velocity of the bullets was so powerful his body was propelled backward into the wall, which prevented him from slumping to the floor. Sincere stepped over to Moose, who was still unconscious on the floor and shot him once in the temple. Moose jerked a few times then became perfectly still. The other men in the apartment thought they were about to meet the same fate. They wasted no time copping pleas. A skinny, brown skinned, young man with an afro yelled, "Blob, we ain't got nothing to do with that shit. Them niggas got what they had called for."

"I want the rest of you niggas to empty yo pockets," Sincere barked. Sincere went from man to man, only taking their IDs. "Now I know where to find you pussies. Talk to five-o, and I'm gonna run up in yo mama's house and rear-range her wig. Do I make myself clear?" Sincere yelled. Before anybody could respond, Twin was already escorting his crew out of the death trap.

CHAPTER 11

At 2:30 p.m. the sky was darkly overcast, giving the early evening an appearance of being later than it actually was. Heavy rain continued to descend from the black clouds, flooding the inner-city streets. Blinding flashes of lightning followed by clamorous thunder periodically ignited the gloomy horizon like fireworks on the fourth of July. Libby stood at the window, dreamily peeking through the venetian blinds. She was watching cars splash puddles of rainwater on the sidewalk when a car she recognized skidded to a halt in front of the building.

"So what's on the agenda for yo birthday?" Twin asked Lil Kev before he exited the car.

"Nothin' special. I'm gonna chill at my grandmother's house. Spend some time with my sisters. Renee said they was expecting me."

"Aiight, but if you change yo mind, hit me up, and I'll come scoop you."

"No doubt. Oh yeah, thanks for the leather jacket. I really appreciate it." Lil Kev smiled.

"I know you do, and if you wasn't so homesick, I would've really set it out for you," Twin said.

"You still can." Lil Kev chuckled.

"Get out my car, nigga." Twin laughed, giving Lil Kev a pound. "Happy birthday," Twin said as Lil Kev exited the BMW.

"Here come Kevin. Turn off the lights. Hurry up, Deyla," Libby shouted from the front window with a huge Kool-Aid smile on her pretty, young face.

"Grandma! Grandma!" Deyla screamed. "Kevin's outside!"

"Oh Lord, where did I put those matches?" Lillian uttered, patting her apron pocket. She reached inside the pocket and pulled out a book of matches with dried cake mix on the cover. "Libby," Lillian yelled, "don't open that door until I'm done lighting all fifteen candles."

Lillian had stayed awake half the night baking a three-layer chocolate cake for her grandson's birthday. Chocolate cake was Kevin's favorite, and Lillian intended to surprise him with his very own three-layer deluxe chocolate cake made from scratch. Lil Kev entered the building, briefly pausing inside the hallway to shake rainwater off his umbrella before entering his grandmother's apartment. Lil Kev knocked three times on the door and waited for someone to answer.

"Who is it?" Libby asked as if she didn't have a clue.

"It's Lil Kev. Open the door, girl!"

"Grandma, it's Kevin," Libby yelled.

"Well, open the door and let him in," Lillian responded excitedly.

"First you gotta close your eyes, Kevin," Libby said through the ajar door.

"Close my eyes for what?" Lil Kev smiled. His instincts told him something special was imminent.

"Boy, just close those big pop-eyes before I close this door on you," Libby snapped, opening the door so her brother could enter.

Once inside, Libby immediately placed both hands over her brother's eyes, and she guided him through the dark apartment toward the kitchen where Lillian and Deyla were waiting. "OK, you can open your eyes now," Libby exclaimed, removing her hands from over his eyes. Lil Kev opened his eyes and blinked a few times before his vision focused. He spotted the triple-layer chocolate cake and became overwhelmed with emotions. The impact of what they had done struck him with the force of a sledgehammer. He had not been allowed in Lillian's house ever since she'd discovered narcotics under his bed, which was approximately eight months ago. So his visit had a dual purpose. One, it was his birthday, and two, it was his first visit since the incident that resulted in his eviction. Today was Kevin's birthday, and Lillian baked him a cake to celebrate. Lil Kev took the visit as a possible sign that his grandmother was expressing how much she'd missed his presence. He definitely missed her and his sisters too, but moving back in wasn't in Lil Kev's plan.

Lillian began to sing "Happy Birthday" as Libby and Deyla both smiled and joined in. When the song ended, everybody took turns kissing him. Lil Kev was truly touched and happy for the first time since being away from his sisters.

"Thanks, I appreciate all the love." Lil Kev smiled from ear to ear.

"Boy, hurry up and make a wish so you can blow out those candles," Lillian shouted.

Lil Kev closed his eyes and made his wish. "I wish I could make this moment, surrounded by all this love, last forever," he thought. "I also wish Renee could be here too. Then she wouldn't have no choice but to show me some love." Lil Kev blew out the candles.

"What you wish for?" Deyla asked Kevin.

"He's not supposed to tell you what he wish for, silly," Libby exclaimed.

"Who else wants some cake?" Lil Kev asked, grabbing a knife from the sink. He sliced three pieces of cake, picked up a slice, and chomped into it.

"I know you ain't planning to eat and run, especially in all that rain out there. So you might as well take that jacket off, boy," said Lillian, looking her grandson over with her beefy arms folded across her chest. Lil Kev demolished his slice of cake in three bites. He then proceeded to cut himself another slice. He got up from the table still chewing, unzipped his jacket, took it off, and handed it to Libby.

"What am I supposed to do with that jacket?" Libby asked.

"The same thing you would do if it was yo broke-ass boyfriend's jacket. Hang it up." Lil Kev chuckled.

"Don't get cute, Kevin. You haven't been gone long enough to forget how I used to whip your butt. And where did you get that chain from?" Libby asked.

"Wow! It's beautiful, Kevin. Is it real?" asked Deyla.

"I got it from Twin, my homey, for my birthday. Yeah, it's real. I don't wear slum jewelry."

"What's slum, Kevin?" asked Deyla.

"Fake jewelry," said Lil Kev, shaking his head from side to side. "Now miss me with all the questions. I didn't come here for that. I came to chill out, and I didn't come empty-handed either. I got gifts for both of y'all." Lil Kev smiled then reached inside the front pocket of his jeans.

"Kevin, it's your birthday, not ours. But we ain't about to turn down no gifts. Right, Deyla?" Libby exclaimed.

"Yup," Deyla responded, smiling from ear to ear.

"Yo, from this point on, we gonna celebrate like it's yo birthday every time I get to be with y'all."

"Yeah right," said Libby in a low, dubious voice. Lil Kev pulled his hand out of his pocket, revealing a huge knot of money. He started fanning himself with the bills, complaining about the temperature inside the apartment with a stoic face. When Libby and Deyla saw all those twenties and fifties, the smiles on their faces froze and simultaneously melted into sober expressions.

Lil Kev witnessed the comical metamorphosis and exploded in laughter. He peeled off four fifty-dollar bills, and he gave them both one hundred dollars. Libby and Deyla had never seen so much money before at one time.

"Boy, I know you don't have a job, and you ain't old enough to play the Lottery. So how did you get that money?" Libby asked, looking at her brother suspiciously. "I hope ain't nobody looking for you for taking this money, Kevin."

"Libby, stop tripping. You jumping the gun, sis. I would never put y'all in harm's way. Where this money came from ain't important. What's important is that there's more where this came from, and I'm gonna give both of y'all some every time we get the chance to be together. Now stop worrying, OK."

"Kevin, you rich?" Deyla asked, still looking at the fifty-dollar bills in her hand.

"Nah, lil sis. I ain't rich yet, but I'm gonna be. Now both of y'all put that money away before Grandma sees it and has a fuckin' conniption. And don't spend it all in one place. Now can a brother get some love?" Lil Kev asked, looking from sister to sister.

He extended his arms wide enough to hug them both at the same time. "I love y'all to life," he whispered.

"We love you too," both girls responded simultaneously.

"Kevin, we want you to come back home," Deyla said, teary eyed. "Ask Grandma if you can you come back home. You want me to ask her for you?" Deyla asked, wiping away tears with the back of her hand.

It broke Lil Kev's heart to see his sisters suffer at his expense. "Listen, it's too late for me to backtrack now, but one day you'll understand that there comes a time when you don't have no choice but to move on. Regardless of the circumstance. Big sis, listen to me," said Lil Kev, trying to convey his message as soothingly as possible, "even if Grandma did agree to let me come back home, it wouldn't be that simple."

"No, Kevin—"

"Libby, hold up."

"No, Kevin. Why?" Libby asked, her voice shaky.

"Because."

"Because what?" Libby countered.

"Because I'm no longer the innocent little boy y'all knew before I flew out the nest. I done been exposed to all kinds of corrupt shit, and I'm not trying to break Grandma's heart again. But don't worry. That ain't gonna stop me from coming by to check on y'all."

"Promise, Kevin?" Libby asked, starting to tear up again.

"Yeah, I promise. Now let me go. I can't breathe. Y'all are choking me."

"Don't forget our gifts when you come by to check on us," Deyla exclaimed, wrapping her arms tightly around his waist. Deyla wouldn't release her hold on Lil Kev.

Lil Kev stared at his little sister as if she had three eyeballs in her head. "She's digging for gold," he thought, grabbing his pockets. Deyla burst out laughing. Libby just shook her head with a big smile on her face.

CHAPTER 12

It was business as usual on the South Side low end. It was the first of the month, so Twin decided to open shop early. His proclivity to make a killing was always stronger on the first of the month than any other day, because everybody had money on the first. It was one of those hot, sultry days in Chicago. The Sun hovered over the horizon.

The poison crew had been pumping dope for five hours straight and killing it. They didn't even want to take their usual break to go get something to eat for fear of missing some money. So they improvised by sending dope fiends out on errands for sandwiches, sodas, candy bars, and cigarettes. When one of them had to take a leak, they pissed between parked cars, right on the block. Blob took it a step further. He sent to the store for a roll of toilet paper, and to everyone's surprise, he proceeded to take a shit in the living room of the abandoned building they used to stash some of their dope. The first of the month was definitely Independence Day for all welfare recipients in and around the community. That check was equivalent to a jug of ice water in the hot Sahara Desert. The average nigga who was accustomed to being broke became self-sufficient on the first.

The cash flow seemed endless. Dope fiends were coming out of the woodwork to get their hands on some poison. Zulu and Lil Kev were working the north end of the block with Blob posted up close by on security. Cee Allah and Black Sun were controlling the south end with trigger-happy Sincere lurking in a doorway on the opposite side of the street. He was dressed in his trademark army fatigues, itching for some action. Twin was also in attendance. He was parked in the middle of the block listening to the rap group Do or Die and politicking with a red bone chick by the name of Sensation.

Every now and again, Twin would drive through the hood, trying to spot an unfamiliar face or someone who looked suspect. Most importantly he was looking for undercover cops. Twin had only known Sensation for approximately three weeks. They met at a strip club called Booty Trap where Sensation was employed as a dancer. She went against her better judgment and allowed Twin the rare opportunity to get to know her intimately. Twin had never seen a stage performance like the one Sensation gave that night.

The female that entered the stage before Sensation was absolutely repulsive. She had crackhead stamped all over her.

She was tall and lanky with small, shriveled up tits that resembled California raisins.

The hue of her dark, ashy skin looked like used charcoal. Her bloodshot eyes were bulging out of her head as if she'd just seen a ghost lurking among the shocked audience. She came out and did a ridiculous cheerleader split that ended with a loud fart. She lay on her back and started scissoring her skinny legs in the air. Rolling onto her stomach, she slithered onto her hands and knees doggy style. Then she tried to make her narrow booty clap. The audience's suspicion was confirmed. While in the middle of her circus act, she reached inside her loosely fitting, knee-high, black leather boots and pulled out a loaded stem and a red Bic lighter. She took a blast right on stage. Twin stood horror-struck and watched as security pounced on top of the crackhead dancer and drug her off the stage. Twin was on his way out of the club when he heard the crowd get excited. They started to applaud. He looked back and saw a fine red bone had come on stage. He immediately made a beeline toward the stage with a drink in hand to get a closer look. Twin had been inside just about every strip club in and around the city, but he'd never witnessed such an erotic performance before.

"Fuck tact and diplomacy," Twin thought. He felt like pouncing on stage and jack rolling her for the pussy at gunpoint. That wasn't his modus operandi, though. However, Twin stood beside the stage sporting a raging hard-on. He was fantasizing about blowing Sensation's back out. While she continued to twist her topless body into a pretzel, she went on to demonstrate every erotic position in that seventies poster calendar. Twin was mesmerized by her unusual and sexual body contortions. He was struggling to maintain his composure. His hands were draped down in front of his crotch in a feeble attempt to cover his throbbing erection. By the time Sensation reached the conclusion of her flaming hot routine, Twin was madly in lust and extremely aroused. Before Sensation left the stage, she surprised everyone in attendance by giving a thunderous round of applause with her forty-two-inch backside. After the standing ovation and catcalls subsided, Twin got Sensation's attention by sticking a fifty-dollar bill inside her black and red G-string. He whispered over the music that there was more where that came from. Twin and Sensation eventually arrived at the VIP room where he didn't waste any time pin cushioning her with an endless supply of dollar bills. He couldn't keep his hands off her body. He groped every inch of her voluptuous frame.

Sensation could see Twin had obviously consumed too much alcohol. When he started rhyming about her appearance and how she was making him feel, she began to loosen up. She sat in Twin's lap and listened to him rhyme.

"What's up, sweet thing? You look like a wet dream. Whoever hit you with the handle Sensation gave you the right name. It complements your sexy frame. One more thang, I like the way yo booty swing. Wish I could take you outta this strip club, and put you on the *Soul Train*. No strings attached.

You don't even have to get naked for that. I'm tryin' to get blessed. I guarantee I got what it takes to satisfy the opposite sex. Fuck the tricks. I want the treats. Yeah, I like dark meat, but I also got a fetish for red bone bitches with pretty feet. Damn, Sensation, you got a fat ass, but you also got class. Got me tryin' to figure you out like calculus math. So what's it gonna be, Sensation? You got my heart racing sitting on my lap with all this ass. What you think, I won't take it?"

Twin stood Sensation up in front of him. He spun her around and palmed her ass.

"That was very good. I'm impressed," said Sensation.

After consuming a bottle and a half of Dom Pérignon and blowing a hundred fifty dollars in one-dollar bills, Sensation reluctantly submitted to Twin's persistent invasion of her lower extremities. When she felt him sliding her G-string to the side, she decided he'd been more than generous and deserved a shot at the title. She abruptly stopped resisting his sexual advances and allowed him to slowly penetrate her in the middle of a steamy lap dance. After that first rendezvous at club Booty Trap, Sensation had remained in contact with Twin, and she made herself available whenever he desired her company.

Twin drove up on Blob and motioned for him to come to his car. "Listen, folks, if y'all wanna take a break and get something to eat, go ahead. In fact, take an hour, aiight? I should be back by then. That's if I don't overindulge in all this candy." Twin chuckled, palming one of Sensation's thighs.

Blob stooped down and peered through the window. He gasped when he saw Sensation sitting in the passenger seat and gyrating seductively to the lyrics of Do or Die.

"I feel you, nigga, 'cause I'm getting a sweet tooth just from lookin'. Do she taste as good as she look?" Blob asked Twin in a low tone.

"Even better. She melts in yo mouth," Twin responded, noticing the naked lust in Blob's eyes as he licked his pink and black lips.

"Is this a private party, folks?" Blob asked, still using a low tone so only Twin could hear him.

"Blob, there's a time and place for everything. If I'm correct, you got business to take care of out here. How you gonna do two things at once? Secure the crew with yo pants down and yo dick out? Listen, when y'all get back, make sure you let Sincere know they can take an hour. All right?" It appeared Blob didn't comprehend because he was paying more attention to Sensation than Twin. He was undressing her with his eyeballs. "Yo, nigga. Did you hear what I said?" Twin barked.

"Yeah, yeah. I heard you," Blob exclaimed, standing back up.

The effect Sensation had on Blob caused Twin to laugh. Twin shook his head and pulled off. Blob told Zulu and Lil Kev he had to holler at Sincere, and then he instructed them to shut down and meet him back on the block in one hour or later. After making sure they understood his instructions, Blob headed down the opposite end of the block to get with

Sincere, his partner in crime. Sincere saw Blob coming down the block. He stepped out from the cover of the doorway to greet Blob.

"Is there a problem? What's wrong?" Sincere asked.

"Nah, everything's good. Breathe easy," Blob replied.

"Then why you ain't on post?"

"Cause Twin gave us a break. He said for y'all to take an hour after us."

"Why? Why he do that?"

"Because the nigga goin' to get his dick wet. He got this badass red bone chick in his car."

"Blob, why is it that every bitch you see is bad?"

"Because, nigga, on a scale of one to ten, this bitch is a hundred. Real talk. What's good, though?" Blob asked.

"Ain't nothing good. It's bad breaks and short stakes. I can reach up and still touch bottom," Sincere exclaimed.

"Yeah, well, that's about to change. I got a sweet sting lined up for us. Yo, you know that tall, dick-sucking bitch, Vanessa, right?"

"Yeah, I know her," said Sincere. "Who don't know that bitch?"

"Well, she leaked some info last week that I followed up on."

"What kind of info?" Sincere asked. "She told me about some older dude getting major paper on the South Side. She also said he's a freak, and he likes wearing female panties and shit. I already know the nigga's routine and where he rest at.

So we don't gotta trunk him, because he keeps everything in his house."

"If he's gettin' the kind of paper you described, then the nigga's foolish to keep that shit where he rest at," said Sincere. "What kind of product does he sell?"

"The same shit we sale. Dog food, weight. So you already know what kind of paper he got. I followed the nigga a few times. He got some nice mutherfuckin' ships too. He also got a quenchless thirst for the taste of pussy. That's his weakness. That's what makes him vulnerable," said Blob.

"Damn, now that sounds like somebody else I know," laughed Sincere.

"Fuck you," Blob replied. "Like I was saying, the nigga's got this grandiose persona about him. It's as if he owns the world and shit. Like he's content about every mutherfuckin' thing. I hope he have that same attitude when we run down on him, because it's gonna work to our advantage. That type of display numbs a nigga's ability to detect danger, and we're gonna exploit it," Blob concluded. He stared at his partner in crime, waiting for Sincere to say something.

Sincere peered at Blob and smiled. "I see you did yo homework."

"Does that mean it's a green light?" Blob asked.

"What's already understood needs no explanation."

"Good," Blob smirked. "I'll get back to you when the opportunity presents itself," said Blob, and then he continued down the block.

CHAPTER 13

Forty-fifth and King Drive was cluttered with pedestrians and vendors on both sides of the street selling food and cold drinks. A fleet of organized vehicles with homemade platforms floated up the street, seemingly defying gravity. Today was the annual parade. Different bands marched along King Drive with rhythmic strides. They were in step with each other and pounding on bass and snare drums. Some blew on trumpets and trombones. Young men and women in drill squads would stop marching periodically to demonstrate military-style drill exhibitions. Teenage girls dressed in black skirts and white go-go boots marched in formation and twirled batons in the air. Most of the male spectators wore colorful short sets, while some of their counterparts, provocatively dressed in wraparound miniskirts and booty-choking daisy dukes, pushed babies around in strollers.

There were lots of spontaneous behaviors. It was as if an aphrodisiac had been released in the air, arousing sexual desires. Everywhere couples were kissing, hugging, groping, and flirting. It made no difference if the people were married or single. Everyone mingled, and the old folk were included. Mayor Daily was also in attendance. He was riding on top of a monstrous red, white, and blue float in statuesque form, waving at the Chicago natives. Dressed mostly in blue, with baseball caps cocked to the sides of their heads, the notorious GDs (Gangster Disciples) threw up gang signs and embraced each other. The Vice Lords and El-Rukins were also live in color, representing and spreading love. Weed smoke permeated the air like toxic fumes from the muffler on a stolen hoopty. Coolers filled to the brim with intoxicating beverages were everywhere. Lillian lived on Forty-fifth and King Drive, which was smack-dab in the middle of the festivities. The parade marched right past her apartment building. Her front porch provided ringside seats. Every year, two or three weeks before the parade, people would offer Lillian money and gifts in exchange for a reserved seat on her porch. Watching the parade from the shelter of her porch was more suitable than standing for hours and having to deal directly with the immense crowd of spectators. Lillian and Charlie's chairs were adjacent to each other, which was Lillian's strategic way of monitoring Charlie's liquor consumption. Lillian was well aware Charlie was on his fourth glass of corn liquor because she had poured it for him. She also knew his tolerance for alcohol was high, and he didn't reach inebriation until his sixth or seventh glass, which was exactly why she kept score.

Every time Charlie's glass reached the point of absolute emptiness, he started to shift around in his chair until he got her attention. Then he would glance down at the jug of moonshine underneath her chair. Someone observing Charlie's behavior for the first time would think he was on the verge of having a fit by the way his eyeballs danced around in their sockets.

As soon as Lillian became aware of his dire need for another taste, she would reach under the chair, grab the jug, and pour him another glass. Lillian was in a good mood from being surrounded by family and friends and, of course, the substantial increase in profits from liquor sales. This was a direct result of the enormous influx of spectators come out to celebrate the parade. People that hadn't seen one another in years were embracing, conversing, and having a wonderful time. Some of Chi-Town's legendary pimps rolled around the outskirts of the parade on custom-made three-wheel tricycles, drinking Moet and Dom Pérignon straight out of the bottle. They were decorated in colorful tailored suits from Fox Brother's and B&B's tailor shops. Full-length fur coats hung loosely from their shoulders like superficial capes despite the eighty-five-degree temperatures. Their customary diamond pinky rings were immense and had a blinding effect on the naked eye every time the afternoon sunlight ricocheted off the surface of those precious stones. Spectators seemed more interested in watching the pimps showboat than the parade exhibition. Everywhere a pimp was spotted, two or three women were in his company listening attentively to every word that escaped his mouth. Each and every one of them was in hot pursuit of new prostitutes. In an endeavor to outshine each other, hoes were paying off like Las Vegas slot machines. Pimps were chasing hoes on tricycles with water guns, others were posing for photos, and some pitched pennies to pass the time at one hundred dollars a pop. (If the penny landed on the line, it paid double.) Fat Louie worked his way through the multicultural crowd of excited spectators, effortlessly firing his cannon on victim alter victim. Fat Louie was a Chicago native. He lives on Forty-seventh Street and Michigan Ave, which was only a hop, skip, and leap from where the parade was taking place. Fat Louie had a very unique occupation. He was a cannon (a professional pickpocket). Although he was born and raised in Chicago, and he learned how to reach at the early age of thirteen, he plied his trade all around the United States. Fat Louie's name rang like Catholic church bells in Rome amongst the elite circle of renowned thieves.

In New York and every other major city in the States, if he was in town, Louie always showed up at the parade. He profited from doing so, but Louie attended the events more out of tradition. Every year he felt more reluctant to work the parade his mother had faithfully brought him to when he was a kid. Fat Louie, though, was a thief and a pickpocket. He was attracted to large crowds and unable to resist the allure of easy pickings.

Louie was also personally responsible for turning out a crew of ambitious young pickpockets from the South Side of Chicago called the Whiz Kids. Over the years these Whiz Kids were directly responsible for the CTA (Chicago Transit Authority) becoming unsafe for upper-, middle-, and even lower-class taxpaying citizens to board a bus, train, or plane without the risk of losing their wallets in the process. These kids continued to wreak havoc on the citizens of Chicago for decades before migrating to New York City with Fat Louie. After relocating to the Rotten Apple and pillaging their tax-payers for the first five years, the anticrime pickpocket squad became alarmed. Larceny and forgery crimes were suddenly a pandemic.

The NYPD had never received so many complaints for the same crime before the arrival of Fat Louie and the Chi-Town Whiz Kids. With over thirty years of experience in the art of dipping, Louie had mastered his craft. Being conspicuously obese, one wouldn't believe how light and swift his hands were. The problem was his hands were too quick for the naked eye to detect. Fat Louie was more comfortable reaching into a victim's pocket than his own. It was rumored he'd once erased the red dot off the forehead of a Hindu without the slightest detection. Louie usually worked with a team, but today, at the parade, he worked solo. He patiently waited for an equally fat white victim to complete his purchase of three jumble hot dogs and an ice-cold can of soda pop at one of the congested concession stands. The fat man finished paying for his food and returned his wallet to his front pocket. He took two steps away from the concession stand with both arms extended in the air, holding the food and drink above his head, while squeezing through the crowd.

With precise timing Fat Louie stepped directly in front of his victim's path, cutting off his movement and stalling the victim. With his Armani suit jacket draped over his right shoulder, matador style, to obscure the play from being witnessed by wandering eyeballs, he dipped into the victim's left front pocket with surreptitious stealth, scissoring the man's billfold between his index and middle finger and quickly depriving him of his wallet. When the play was over, Fat Louie faded into the oblivious crowd fifteen hundred dollars richer and in search of his next victim.

The rowdy group of adolescents had been following her for approximately six blocks, whistling and catcalling to the gorgeous actress while she rode on top of the pink and white feathery float. Dressed in a blue two-piece bathing suit and waving at the fans, she was absolutely breathtaking. Observing the parade from his grandmother's porch, Lil Kev noticed the commotion around the pink and white float.

Curious, he stood on his chair to get a closer look at the lady who was riding the float in the powder blue bikini with the Angela Davis afro and attracting so much attention. Lil Kev almost fell out of his chair when he recognized her. His mouth fell open. "It can't be," he thought.

"Oh shit. Yes the fuck it is," he mumbled. It was Thelma from the popular 70s sitcom, *Good Times*. She was on top of a float in the Chicago Parade, live and in the flesh. Lil Kev leaped off Lillian's porch, pushing and shoving his way through the crowd of infatuated fans.

"Yo, move out the fuckin' way," he growled as he forced his way through the crowd toward the attractive actress. Lil Kev caught up to the float and extended his hand. "Hi, Thelma. I'm Lil Kev. You look even better in person than you do on TV," he exclaimed in a counterfeit Billy D. Williams voice.

She shook his hand, smiled, and said, "Thanks for the compliment, Lil Kev." Still smiling she continued, "Thelma's not my real name. That's the character I play. My name is Bernadette."

"Oh, is that right?" Lil Kev asked. Billy D. Williams had taken a leave of absence. He was now speaking in his true voice. "Bernadette, would you mind giving me your autograph?"

"Of course not. Do you have something I can write on?" Bernadette asked, rummaging through her pocketbook for a pen. Lil Kev dug in his pocket and fished through his money for the largest bill in his bankroll. He was trying hard to impress the gorgeous celebrity with big shot antics.

"Here you go, baby girl. Write on this," he said, passing her a one hundred-dollar bill. She autographed the bill and passed it back to Kev. He thanked her with a wink and headed back toward the porch. Everybody on Lillian's porch witnessed the theatrics, except Mr. Charlie, who had finally passed out in his chair from an overdose of corn liquor.

CHAPTER 14

The stolen gray Maverick slowly cruised past a huge brick house with a well manicured lawn, and it parked three houses down in a quiet residential neighborhood.

"He's home. That's one of his cars. That black berg parked in the driveway. The TV's on in the front room. Somebody's in there," the husky dark-skinned young hoodlum in the passenger seat whispered. He reeked of alcohol and sounded inebriated. The driver glanced over at his partner in crime with a serious expression. His frown contracted his eyebrows. He was gritting his teeth and flexing his jawbone. He reached in his waistband and pulled out a chrome .45 automatic handgun, checked the clip, and then said in a frigid voice, "Yeah, folks, I can see that somebody's inside the house, but that's my least concern right now. I'm more concerned about something else."

Curious, Blob shifted in his seat and whispered, "Oh yeah? And what is that?"

"What is that?" Sincere whispered, intentionally mimicking Blob. "That's a beautiful question, but I'd rather hear the answer. Explain to me why yo black ass keep whispering. We the only two mutherfuckas inside this car. Nigga, are you on drugs? What the hell is the matter with you? Whatever's got you tripping, you need to put that shit on freeze so we can handle our business. I need to know I can count on you. Feel me?"

Blob stared at his partner in crime as if he'd just asked him if he could palm his ass. "Nah, I don't feel you, nigga. Miss me with that bullshit you talking. Yeah, I had something to drink before you scooped me, but that ain't shit. You know you can count on me. I'm still the same, nigga. I ain't tripping. Shit, I didn't know I was whispering. Why you ain't tell me?"

Sincere glanced at his wristwatch. It reads 3:38 a.m. "Nigga, come on. Let's go collect our money."

Sincere's beady eyes resembled a venomous viper. He pulled the hoodie over his head. Blob followed suit. Both hoodlums exited the Maverick and headed toward the house with the black Benz in the driveway.

Her sleep was suddenly invaded by the loud, piercing sound of a car alarm. She yawned, rolled over on her back, and began to squint at the ceiling through partly closed eyes. She struggled to clear her vision and shake the lethargy. She was confused and didn't recognize where she was at until she glanced over at the enormous figure lying next to her sound asleep. Then it all began to make sense. Now fully aware of her surroundings, with only one hour of shut-eye under her belt, the promiscuous gold digger could still feel the lingering effects of too much Dom Pérignon, Rémy Martin, Buddah Bless, and raw fishscale they had sniffed. Last night she threw caution to the wind and got so fucked up that her clothes weren't the only thing that came off. So did her dignity. Sugar Bear, being the snake he was, could sense Renee's vulnerability. At her weakest point, he stuck without warning, shattering what little was left of her invisible shield.

Caught in his web of aggressive persuasion and sadistic manipulation, she became totally submissive. She even encouraged him, which she regretted immediately. Bear was brutal. He ignored her pleas to end the abuse. Despite the tears and relentless protesting, Bear continued to pound savagely in and out of her rectum until he felt a powerful orgasm approaching. He yanked his manhood out of Renee's tight asshole and released a huge load of semen all over her beefy ass cheeks. Renee leaped off the bed in pain, feeling humiliated, and she ran to the bathroom to prepare a hot bath. She let her guard down, and Sugar Bear seized the opportunity to take what Renee had once vowed to never let a man experience the pleasure of taking from her: the brown eye. Bear also took the liberty of secretly filming the entire sex show. Exhausted from last night's rendition, Renee glanced at the gold Movado watch on her wrist. It read 3:45 a.m.

"Bear, wake up. Get up, Bear," Renee groaned, shoving him with her elbow.

"What? What's going on?" Bear mumbled in a groggy, irritated tone. "What is it?"

"It's your car alarm. Something must've triggered it, and it's driving me insane. Get up, and go shut it off."

"What?" Bear grumbled, lifting up on one arm. He stared at Renee through slits of bloodshot eyes, which reflected too much partying and not enough rest. "What the fuck is going on," he thought, reluctantly getting out of bed. He grabbed his silk robe and proceeded toward the front door barefoot.

Outside Blob and Sincere were posted on the porch. They both had their backs glued to the wall on both sides of the door when it suddenly swung open. The threshold of the door was as far as Bear got. Blob popped off the wall like a jack-in-the-box.

He was aiming the .357 Magnum at Sugar Bear's forehead. "Get the fuck back inside," Blob sneered, forcing Bear back inside his house. Sincere ran back down the stair to the car. He reached under the hood, and the car alarm abruptly stopped screaming.

He raced back up the stairs, taking them two at a time. He was extremely excited things were going as planned. He entered the house with his gun in hand. He closed the door and locked it. A delightful smile appeared on his face when he saw Blob had their victim seated on the plush carpet floor, still aiming his .357 at Bear's head. "Who else is in this house, mutherfucka?" Sincere barked, pointing his weapon at Bear.

"Just a lady friend of mine," Bear responded, glancing from one man to the other with scorn. The TV was on, but the screen was blank. An annoying beeping sound was emitting from the set. "Damn, I'm caught slipping," Bear thought. "How the fuck did I get caught in a blizzard naked? God, please don't let this be my last day breathing."

Bear couldn't think straight. He struggled to recall what day it was, but he couldn't remember. His eyes were blood-shot red. He was hungover with a migraine. He felt absolutely powerless. He willed himself to get focused. He made the two gunmen his personal subjects of scrutiny. He locked them on his radar, searching for something, anything, recognizable that could help him later identify the brazen bastards that had the audacity to invade the one place designed to provide security, his home.

Sugar Bear began to silently pray. "God, please protect me. Help me make it through this whole ordeal with my life. Anything else, God, can be replaced."

"Nigga, where the fuck is that bitch?" Sincere growled, cocking his gun.

"Down the hall in my bedroom sleeping. The door's open," Bear uttered with disdain.

"I'm on it!" Blob said. His voice was just above a whisper. Sincere shot him a look that implied he needed to stay focused, which Blob quickly acknowledged with a slight head nod. He cocked the .357 Magnum and began to creep down the hallway toward Sugar Bear's bedroom.

Renee quickly dozed back off to sleep after Sugar Bear got out of bed to shut off the car alarm. Currently she was with Morpheus (the Greek god of dreams). She was stretched out in bed and lying on her stomach, naked except for a tiny, see-through, vanilla-colored negligee. Her long, smooth, curvaceous legs were parted, leaving her bare vagina exposed.

Blob entered the bedroom with his gun extended in front of him. "Damn," he gasped, staring between Renee's thighs. His dick started to rise instantly. "What a beautiful sight," he thought. The crotch of his pants poked out. He uncocked his gun and subconsciously rubbed his crotch. He was quietly tiptoeing toward the bed to get a better look. The close-up view of Renee's shaved vagina snatched Blob's breath away. He leaned forward to get an even closer look. The sight of Renee's gorgeous, spread-eagle body ignited a fire in Blob's loin that only a shot of her irresistible pussy could put out. Consumed with lust and the overwhelming desire to dip his manhood in her outweighed any rational thought. Still bending forward with his face now only inches away from Renee's pussy, Blob unzipped his pants. He pulled out his erection and proceeded to climb on the bed and straddle Renee's exhausted body. He began to fondle her lower extremities. Renee stirred tiredly and began to protest.

"Stop, Bear. Get off me. I'm still fuckin' sore." Her words were abruptly cut off by what felt like the cold end of a gun barrel pressed against the side of her head. Her eyes shot open. She used her peripheral vision and was able to recognize a big gun pressed against her temple along with a vague image of someone wearing a dark hoodie. "Bear!" Renee screamed.

"Bitch, shut the fuck up," Blob sneered, slapping Renee on the side of her face with his free hand. "Go ahead, bitch. Scream again. I double dare you. Scream again, and I'm gonna blow yo brains all over yo pillow."

As soon as Sincere heard the commotion, he yelled, "Folks, talk to me."

"Everything's good. I got this," Blob yelled back. He was aiming his weapon between Renee's legs and trying to penetrate her from behind.

"Let's go. Get the fuck up," Sincere barked to Bear. Bear led the way as he and Sincere made their way toward Bear's bedroom. As soon as they reached the bedroom, Sincere shoved Bear into the room and made him sit on the floor. The action taking place on the bed snatched Sincere's attention. "Get the fuck off that bed, folks," Sincere snapped at his partner in crime.

Blob looked over his shoulder and held up five fingers. "Just five minutes. That's all I need, folks."

"Nigga, I'm not gonna tell you again. Get down or get laid down. We came for the money, not the honey."

Blob reluctantly put his deflated dick back inside his pants and smacks Renee on her beefy ass cheeks. He climbed off the bed.

"Here, take this," said Sincere, tossing Blob a roll of duct tape. "Restrain that nigga."

Blob quickly duct-taped Sugar Bear's wrists, ankles, and mouth. He started toward Renee to tape her, but Sincere stopped him dead in his tracks. Sincere didn't want his freak ass nowhere near the exotic looking lady. Sincere had to struggle to stay focused himself as he restrained Renee. "Damn, this bitch is the truth," he thought. He shook out of the fog of her magnetic pull and turned to Bear. He said, "If you can hear me, nod yo head."

Bear nodded his head.

"Good, 'cause I'm not gonna repeat myself. If you value life, pay close attention and listen to the question I'm about to ask you. It's a simple question that deserves a simple answer. Where's the stash at? All of it?"

Blob leaned down and ripped the duct tape off Bear's mouth so he could speak. "Listen, brothers, y'all obviously picked the wrong house. I'm not a drug dealer. Now if y'all are pressed for cash, which is obvious, my wallet's on top of the dresser. There's about eighteen or nineteen hundred dollars in there. Take it. It's yours. Just leave my house, please."

"Tape his mouth back up. He thinks we playin' games," Sincere said to Blob.

Blob shook his head and replaced the tape on Bear's mouth.

"Find the kitchen, and turn the gas on in this mutherfucka," Sincere barked at Blob. Bear started shaking his head franticly from side to side and moaning through the tape.

"What, nigga?" Sincere growled. He snatched the tape off Bear's mouth.

"The stash is in the closet inside a gray and black hatbox. That's on the real." Sincere motioned for Blob to go retrieve the hatbox. Blob entered the closet and immediately spotted the hatbox on top of the shelf. He reached up and grabbed the box, opened it, and discovered half a key of heroin and two rubber band stacks of one hundred-dollar bills.

"Bingo," he yelled. On his way out of the closet, he helped himself to a butterscotch colored leather jacket. Blob yanked the jacket off a hanger and exited the walk-in closet with the leather jacket folded over his arm and the hatbox in his hand. He stepped toward Sincere and lifted the lid so Sincere could see what was inside. Sincere nodded his approval and then turned to Bear. "You surprise me, stupid motherfucka. Your stash can be replaced. Your life can't." He swung his gun at Bear's head, knocking him out cold.

Renee was shaking like a pair of craps dice. She believed she was next to feel the wrath of Sincere's gun. When she saw the two thugs making their exit, she breathed a sigh of relief. She just wanted to get out of Bear's house and go home. Bear regained consciousness and freed himself. Then he took the tape off of Renee. "Them motherfuckas are dead in the water!"

"How are they dead, Bear? You don't even know them bastards," Renee retorted.

"Yeah, but it won't be hard to find out who they are. The nigga that hit me with the gun, the slim dude, has a pitchfork tattoo on the back of his hand, and the fat freak motherfucka had a bull dog charm around his neck. I'm gonna fix them niggas. Watch." Bear grabbed the phone and dialed a number. "Yeah, John. It's Bear."

"Yo, Twin, where we on our way to?" Lil Kev asked from the passenger seat.

"To Heaven on Earth, nigga!" Twin said, passing Lil Kev the joint. "And guess what?" Twin continued. "You don't have to die to get there."

Twin and Lil Kev were on their way to Twin's mother's house. Mrs. Washington had heard so much about Lil Kev, and she was eager to meet him. Normally Twin wouldn't dare bringing anyone to his mother's house, but when he protested, his mother insisted.

"'Sup, Mommy?" said Twin, giving his mother a hug. "This is Lil Kev who I been telling you about."

"Hi, son, nice to finally meet you. How are you?"

"I'm fine, Mrs. Washington. It's good to meet you too," said Kev.

"Maurice has told me so much about you. I just had to invite you to my house."

"I hope what he told you about me was all good."

"Why wouldn't it be?"

"Come on, Kev," Twin said, pulling him away from his mother before she had the chance to get personal. "Let me show you around."

After they toured the house and ate, Twin took Lil Kev to the basement where they smoked weed and watched videos. Twin went to the back of the basement and came back dragging a footlocker. He opened it and began removing books. Underneath the books was where the weapons were stashed. Kev was in awe. Twin pulled out two Twin Glocks, 9 mms.

"I call them the twins." He passed them to Lil Kev. Kev aimed both guns at the video vixen on the TV screen. "This right here," Twin said, pulling out a pump-action shotgun "is the crowd-pleaser. This motherfucka here, this Uzi, it speaks for itself. It's the Windy City typewriter." Twin stepped into the laundry room and showed him the contents. There was $93,000 wrapped in rubber bands and some very expensive jewelry.

"Damn, Twin, I didn't know you was getting it like this."

"Because it wasn't yo business to know until I made it yo business." Twin passed him a piece of paper with the numbers to the safe on it.

"Fuck is this?" Lil Kev asked.

"It's the numbers to that," Twin said, pointing at the safe. "I want you to have it just in case fate stacks the deck against me. All I ask is you make sure my mother is able to maintain the lifestyle she's become accustomed to. Can you promise me that?"

"Yeah, Twin. That's the least I can do. I owe you big time for lookin' out for me. Puttin' me on and shit."

"Listen, Kev. All we got is our world."

CHAPTER 15

It was hot enough to fry an egg on the ground on Chicago's South Side. People were trying to beat the heat by any means necessary. Those that didn't have a way to get to the beach or a pool were utilizing the neighborhood fire hydrants.

Twin was on Fifty-fifth and King Drive at the park where there were three pools in one. He was on the high diving board showboating while his crew remained on the block, selling his product and enduring the heat. They were oblivious to his whereabouts. Twin climbed out of the pool and headed toward his towel. He shook water out of his afro and accidentally showered Renee, who happened to be sitting poolside with her feet dangling in the water.

"Yo be careful with that water. If I wanted to get my hair wet, I would be in the water."

"It was a mistake, and I apologize from the basement of my heart to the balcony of my brain. I'm willing to compensate you for whatever the damage is. But to be honest, all I see is perfection."Twin smiled.

"Let me be the judge of that," said Renee. "What's your name?" she asked, patting her hair.

"My name is Twin."

"Is that the name your mother gave you?"

"Nah, but hopefully it'll suffice for now. What's yo pretty name?"

"My name is Renee."

"Pleased to meet you, Renee."Twin extended his hand.

"Likewise, Twin," Renee uttered, taking his hand. "How old are you?"

"I'm old enough to drive a BMW and control the lives of a young pack of wolves."Twin smiled again.

"What?" Renee asked, her eyebrows crinkling.

"Never mind, let's just say I'm old enough. No disrespect, Renee, but you fine as wine. Slim waist and pretty face. That's just my taste."

"I bet you tell that shit to every woman you speak to."

"Not every women. Only the ones as fine as you."

"Whatever," Renee smirked. She was starting to feel Twin. This young nigga definitely had swagger. "I wonder if he's got paper too," she thought.

"Listen, Renee, I'm not gonna waste anymore of yo time, but I'm about to bounce outta here. If you wanna join me for some fun, all expenses are on me."

"What kind of fun, Twin?" Renee asked.

"Adult entertainment fun. If you with it, then meet me in the parking lot in twenty minutes." Twin stepped off before Renee could respond. Twin sat inside his BMW rolling weed and listening to "I Wanna Rock Right Now" By Rob Base when Renee exited the pool into the parking lot. She looked around and spotted Twin inside his car. She walked toward his car looking like a porn star. Renee was wearing the same pink two-piece bathing suit. The only modification to her scanty attire was a red, silk, see-through scarf wrapped around her waist. Twin was busy rolling weed, so he didn't see Renee until she banged on the window. She was standing next to the passenger door with her hands on her hips. Twin looked up and smiled. He opened the door for her. Renee entered the car and turned her body so she was facing Twin with her back against the passenger door. She deliberately put her left foot on the seat, exposing her fat, scantily clad crotch. Twin zeroed in between her legs and immediately started to drool. Renee had a camel's foot between her legs. Twin hit the joint hard then passed it to Renee. He looked on as she slowly sucked the joint as if it was a miniature cock. Twin removed her sandal and caressed her feet. He fondled her ankle then slowly ran his hand up her leg toward her fat crotch. When Twin's hand was within inches of her vagina, Renee abruptly grabbed his hand, stopping him from going further.

Twin leaned forward and popped open the glove compartment. He pulled out a wad of fifty-dollar bills and dropped six of them on the dashboard. Renee's arm shot out as if guided by a remote control. She swept the bills off the dashboard in one motion and stuffed the bills inside her top. She opened her legs. Twin took the liberty of pulling Renee's bikini to the side, and he caressed her exposed vagina. After he finished having his way with her, they exchanged phone numbers, and he dropped Renee off at her car. Then Twin headed toward the low end where his crew pumped dope. As soon as Twin arrived on the block, his team surrounded his car.

"Where the fuck you been at?" Black Sun asked Twin after he got out of his car and gave everybody a pound.

"I went and took a dip in the pool. What, nigga?" Twin retorted.

"What? You been swimming while we been out here roasting in the heat serving these fiends?" snapped Cee Allah.

"Nigga, you better chill the fuck out. I don't have to explain my whereabouts to you. What the fuck is wrong with you? Better check yo self."

"Watch yo mouth, playboy," Blob said to Cee Allah.

"What up, Twin?" asked Sincere.

"Ain't nothing. Where's Lil Kev?"

"He went to the corner store," said Zulu. "Here he come now."

"What up, Twin?" Lil Kev asked as he approached the crew. He was drinking from a water bottle.

"Ain't nothing, lil nigga. I wish yo ass was with me today. I just finished knocking off this badass old head chick. You missed out, nigga. We could've tossed her up together. I gave the bitch some change, and it was well worth it." Twin shrugged.

Lil Kev shook his head in disgust.

"What the fuck you shaking yo head for?" Blob barked.

"'Cause that's tricking, and I ain't no trick," said Kev.

"It ain't tricking if you got it," said Zulu.

"Nigga, I got it, and I'm gonna keep it," said Lil Kev, flashing a bankroll.

"Yo, Kev, that bitch was the truth. She was fine as hell. Pretty face, little waist, with a fat ass. And she sucked my dick up until I hiccupped."

"Yeah, whatever. It's still tricking. How many you want?" Lil Kev asked a light-skinned dope fiend with freckles on his face.

"Give me two, shorty."

John the Baptise and Sugar Bear had maintained a loyal friendship since they were adolescents. They met inadvertently in Saint Charles, a youth correctional facility.

Bear was being robbed for his weed package by two Vice Lords when John the Baptise intervened. He pulled out a shank he kept inside his Bible and stabbed both of the would-be robbers. Bear showed his appreciation by buying John the Baptise's mother a used car so she could visit her son more often. They had remained close friends into adulthood. John the Baptise had six bodies on Bear's order. Whenever Bear had a problem, he fixed it.

A bum pulling a rusty old wagon with cans loaded on it stopped next to Mittens the Mascot. Mittens worked for the poison crew running customers their way. He was called Mittens because of his swollen hands, which resembled mittens. He was a seasoned dope fiend. He was nodding when the bum approached him.

"Yo," said the bum, "whose shit you had?"

Mitten came out of his nod. "I had poison. It's the best dope in the universe," he said, pointing the bum toward Twin and his crew. They were still on the corner across the street. Twin was still telling his crew about the older lady he fucked. He was posted up with his back to the street.

"Yeah, Kev, you talking that trick shit, but if yo ass was with me, you would've dug in yo pocket too, bad as this bitch was."

The bum walked across the street toward the poison crew. He opened his soiled trench coat as he approached the poison crew. He cradled the sawed-off shotgun hanging from his shoulder by a piece of rope. When he got within range, he yelled, "For what profits a man if he gain the world but lose his soul?" This was followed by a barrage of shotgun blasts. Twin got hit in his back. Lil Kev caught one in the shoulder. Blob and Sincere returned fire as John the Baptise ran up the block and hopped inside the getaway car. Lil Kev cradled Twin in his lap. "Don't die on me, Twin. Fight it, man. You gonna make it. Just hold on."

Twin tried to speak. He was coughing up blood. Lil Kev leaned closer to hear what Twin was saying. "Damn, Lil Kev," Twin said barely audibly, "I always knew living was hard, but

I didn't know dying was this easy. Tell my mother I love her. Tell her I'm sorry. Take care of her for me." Twin coughed up more blood and then took his last breath.

"No, Twin," Kev cried. "Don't leave. I need you, partner."

"Kev, we gotta bounce. Ain't nothing we can do for him. He's gone," said Sincere.

"I'm staying with him. He's the only brother I have," said Lil Kev. The crew heard the police sirens in the distance and started fading into the alley and gangways. "Damn, fate stacked the deck on you, homey," Lil Kev thought.

Reluctantly Kev called Mrs. Washington and broke the news of her son's death.

"Hi, Mom. It's Lil Kev. I need you to come get me."

"Where are you?" she asked.

"I'm at Cook County Hospital."

"Where's my son, Kevin?" Mrs. Washington asked.

"He's in the morgue, Mom," Lil Kev wept.

After Mrs. Washington went to the morgue to claim her son's body with a fellow church member, they picked Lil Kev up and went to her house. It was unusually quiet in the car as they rode to Mrs. Washington's house. When they arrived she put cold chicken in the microwave and served her church friend and Lil Kev. He wolfed down his chicken, feeling uncomfortable in Twin's absence. He went to the basement, took two pain pills, and turned on the videos.

Lil Kev fell asleep and started replaying the episode in his mind that led to Twin's death and his shoulder injury. In his dream he heard a lady yelling, "Not my baby. God, not my son!"

Kev snapped out of his sleep and saw Mrs. Washington rolling around on the floor weeping uncontrollably. He got up and helped her to the couch.

"Kevin, what happened to my son?"

"Mom, we was on the block doing what we do, and this bum motherfucka…excuse me. A bum yelled out, 'for what profits a man if he gains the world but loses his soul?' Then he opened fire on us."

"What kind of person would quote the Bible and then kill my son?"

"I don't know, but when I find out, he's gonna meet his maker."

"Don't talk like that in my house, boy. You got a chance to make something out of your life. It's too late for Maurice. Take his death as a lesson, and make something of yourself."

"Mrs. Washington, I don't expect you to understand the life we live, but if it was me lying in the morgue, I would expect the same of Twin. I'm gonna get the person that did this to my brother. That's the bottom line," said Kev. Tears began to stream down both their faces. "I'm not gonna rest until this is dealt with."

To be continued…

www.ingramcontent.com/pod-product-compliance
Lightning Source LLC
Chambersburg PA
CBHW072229190626
46809CB00017B/1542